A DRAGON'S FATE

THE HIDDEN REALM - BOOK THREE

USA TODAY BESTSELLING AUTHOR

HEATHER RENEE

Contents

DRAGO
THE DARK FOREST
CILLIAN'S HOUSE
NANNIO'S HOUSE
ROCK POINT
THE HIDDEN REALM

MYSTICS

BUCKNER
HALL

CEDAR
HOUSE
COLUMBIA
HOUSE

RAINER
HALL

OLYMPUS
HOUSE
SNAKE
HOUSE

ADAMS
HALL

BAKER
HOUSE
YAKIMA
HOUSE

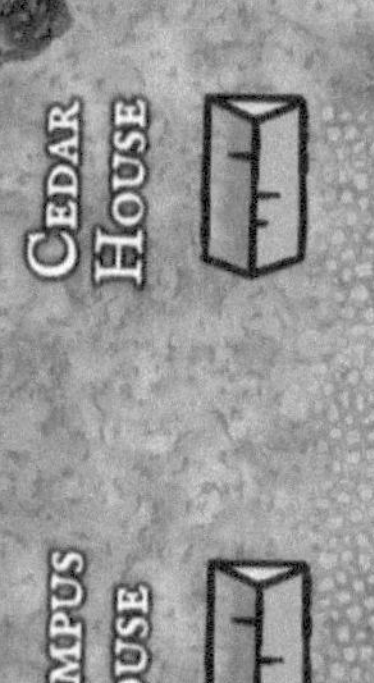

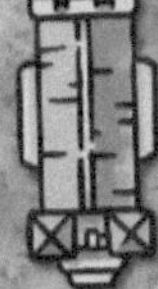
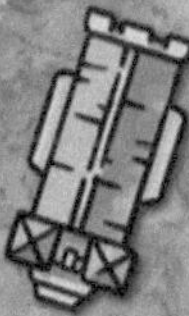
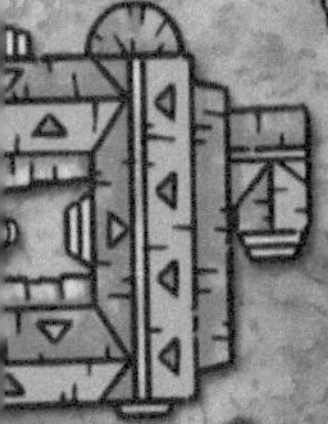
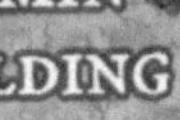

ACADEMY
ING
LL
DragonTail
Hall
PPA'S
ART
Gym
Library
MIN
LDING
Sparks
Cafe
Staff
Housing

Chapter One

DAWSYN

For two days, I'd stayed at Cillian's side as much as I could handle. Two days of putting up with his brooding attitude, his grunts, and his snarls. The time had finally come for me to walk away. For both of our sanities.

Plus, I'd run out of time waiting on him. He wasn't ready to go back to Earth, and I needed to check in with my family before they forced their way through the portal, even if they still thought it could kill them.

My hope was that by leaving Cillian behind in the cave, he'd be able to find some clarity to the shitstorm of emotions he was warring with. It wasn't that I didn't understand. Somewhere between losing our bond and "killing" his brother, my mate had justifiably had enough.

Hell, even I was furious to learn that Knox hadn't actually died. Add that to being told the reason behind his unfortunate not-death… The shitty luck just kept stacking up for us.

Knox wasn't just Cillian's half-brother. He was an Ember dragon, which meant that when he died by the hand of his stronger familial half, he became immortal in a way he wasn't before.

Like I said before. Shitty fucking luck.

Ember dragons were so rare that none of us had reason to suspect it had anything to do with Knox's endgame. Taunting Cillian into killing him so he could claim his ultimate power was completely unexpected.

Though, part of me wondered if that had failed. In the last two days, we hadn't heard a thing from the dark forest or sensed anyone stirring about there.

But Knox and his potentially indestructible qualities were the least of my concern for the moment.

My mate, on the other hand… Cillian had been through hell, and there wasn't a single thing that I could do to help him process his emotions. I'd tried to be there for him, but he didn't want to talk to me—or anyone else, for that matter—which was why I was now walking through the portal back to Earth. On my own.

I had family to check in with and a best friend to put at ease, and if I was being honest with myself, I'd needed some space from all the heaviness in the cave. So, I was going back to Mystics Academy for a few hours.

Based on the plethora of text messages coming through on Cillian's phone once I was back to the Earth side, it was a good thing I'd made the choice to come back.

River wasn't happy with me. I'd told him that I would see him the next day after the fight, but it had been two days without a word from me. He had no problem letting me know he wasn't okay with that.

I stood outside the portal, scrolling through the rest of my messages. My GiGi had let me know she was going to be unavailable for a short time, but that Ava, one of my grandmother's top witches, would be able to help me get where I needed to.

After I sent a text to Ava, asking her to teleport me to Mystics Academy, I took a moment to breathe in the fresh mountain air and enjoy the sun shining down on my face.

There was still snow on the ground, but it was beginning to melt and not nearly as frigid as it had been just a few days ago.

I didn't bother to text River back. He'd only call me to yell, which I imagined he'd do less of if I was standing right in front of him the next time we spoke. It was Saturday, and he'd hopefully be in his dorm when I arrived. Surprising him sounded more enjoyable than having him berate me as soon as he realized I had access to a phone.

Ava's form shimmered into appearance. She was dressed appropriately for the snowy terrain, wearing a thick wool coat, jeans, and boots, yet still shivered, causing her short ebony hair to move over her shoulders.

"Hell, Dawsyn," she complained. "How are you standing out here in jeans and a t-shirt?"

I shrugged and smiled. "Wolf shifter perks." Though,

too much colder and my teeth would have been chattering.

She rolled her light-grey eyes and reached out to grab my forearm. "Let's get out of here."

"You know where—" Before I could finish the question, the world fell out from beneath me then reappeared just as quickly. When I blinked, we were in front of Baker House, the dorm I'd stayed in with River.

My chest heaved as I recalled my couple of weeks at the academy, mostly remembering my last day here, which had been filled with several highs and a massive low once Knox had gotten his hands on me.

"Here." Ava handed me my phone. "Beatrix had this. Told me to give it to you and already added my number. I'm available for you as needed."

There was a slight emphasis on "needed." I was sure GiGi told her she had to take me anywhere I requested, but the witch likely had no desire to be my magical taxi several times throughout the day.

"Thanks, Ava," I said. "I'll be here for a while, then possibly—" Just as I was going to say I may need to go visit my parents, a text came in from my mom on my phone.

Mom: Lucinda is having her baby. Dad and I are headed to Fae Islands. If you need us, we'll be back before you can even finish asking. Let us know how you are as soon as you're able. We love you.

Me: Give Aunt Lucy and Uncle Finn a hug from me and a kiss to the baby when he's here. And I'm okay. Back at the academy before River tries to

hunt me down, then headed back to Drago, but I'll be back again as soon as I can be.

I glanced back at Ava. "I guess it will just be here and back to the portal. I assume Beatrix is unavailable because she's headed to Fae Islands as well?"

The witch nodded. "She left this morning."

I hated that I was missing this moment for my aunt, but I was glad everyone else close to her could be there. Though, I had a fleeting thought to request that my parents didn't tell Aunt Lucy where I was or what I was doing.

Knowing her, she'd be the first in line to obliterate some dragons, but she and Finn deserved to focus only on their baby. I wouldn't be the one to take this time from them.

Ava glanced around, then back to me. "Be careful here, Dawsyn. Beatrix has been mumbling some things, and she's not too pleased with the academy right now."

I'd forgotten about the professor who had the stolen witch book.

"I'll just be in River's dorm," I promised, then held up my phone. "And I'll keep your number at the ready."

With one curt nod, she disappeared and I turned back to Baker House. My feet quickly carried me inside, taking the stairs three at a time until I was at River's door.

I almost knocked until remembering I technically lived there, too.

The handle twisted in my palm just as the door was jerked open and I lost my hold. River was on the other side, chest heaving as he pulled me into his grasp.

"Damn you, Dawsyn," he growled in my ear, holding me tightly. "Two fucking days you made me wait."

"I know. I'm sorry," I said with conviction. "Things didn't quite go as planned."

He pushed me back and appraised my face and arms. "But you're okay? Where's Cillian?"

The concern in his voice when asked about Cillian had my heart expanding.

"I'm good. Just a few bumps and bruises that already healed," I said. "Cillian, on the other hand, isn't quite as good."

River grabbed my hand and pulled me toward the couch after shutting the door behind me. "But he's alive?"

"Yeah. Though, I'm pretty sure he wishes otherwise," I replied. "It hasn't been easy for him since I was taken. He's learned a lot and taken even more hits, both physically and mentally."

I went on to explain about his grandmother working with Knox—though, according to her she was double-crossing Knox, not us; the death of his uncles; finding his father, who had yet to heal from the injuries he'd received the day of the battle courtesy of Knox; and then knowing that by killing his brother, Cillian had ignited a power inside the dragon that seemed nearly impossible to defeat.

Knox had baited Cillian into that fight. He'd wanted —no, needed—to die. Yet, regardless of what their grandmother said, everyone had a weakness. No matter what power they contained. We'd find Knox's, and then we would end him.

River let out a low whistle as I finished. "Shit. No wonder it took you longer to come back here. Hell, I'm surprised you showed up at all."

I leaned my head against his shoulder and sighed. "It was hard to leave Cillian, but I can't fix his heart. Not in the way he currently needs. The only thing I knew I could do was ease your worries."

A crease formed between River's brows as he glanced down at me. "But the bond. Shouldn't you be able to fill him with all kinds of happy shit?"

I'd yet to tell River that by saving him and tying myself to Knox, I'd lost the bond to Cillian. Hope had stayed with me that it would just take time to return, but as the days and hours passed without a flicker of the tether that I'd once shared with Cillian... It was harder to remain hopeful of its return.

"Our bond is gone," I said softly.

He jerked back and turned until he was facing me better. "You actually rejected him? I don't understand."

I shook my head and forced a smile to my face. "No, he's my mate regardless of the bond, but when I broke the connection to Knox, the tether to Cillian didn't return."

"Fuck," he hissed, looking across the room instead of at me. His fingers curled into fists, and he let out a ragged breath. "You shouldn't have gone with Knox to save me."

I grabbed River's shoulders and shook him. "Yes, I should have. Do you think that I could have ever been truly happy with Cillian if I'd let you die? I made the choice that was best for not only you, but for me, and I don't for one second regret any of it."

"You should," he grumbled.

"No," I said sternly. "I love you, River. You're more than my best friend. You're my family. And if you have any love for me at all, then you're going to move on from what happened just like I have. Cillian is still my mate, and I'm his. The bond might have strengthened our connection, but it wasn't the only reason I chose to be with him."

River wrapped his arms around me, hugging me tightly. "I'm so fucking sorry, D."

"It's okay," I murmured against his chest. "You're alive. I have Cillian, and the bond to Knox is gone. Now, we just need to kill him. For good this time."

He jerked back. "I'm going to help you with that."

The conviction not only in his words but his eyes speared my chest. As much as I didn't want River involved, I knew that protecting people was in his DNA. Hell, that was why he was here at Mystics Academy.

I couldn't be so selfish as to keep him from doing what made him *him*.

"Okay," I said.

"Okay? As in 'Yes, River. We'd love to have your help' or more like 'Okay, only in your dreams will I ever let you follow me into another realm'?"

I chuckled at his dramatics. "You can come back with me. Apparently when they lifted the restrictions on the portal, they couldn't put them back. You're safe to join me, and I'm not going to tell you no. Mostly because I wouldn't let you tell me no if the roles were reversed."

He rolled his eyes but hugged me again. "I'm not going to let anything else happen to you. Not again."

Just as I knew Cillian couldn't protect me from everything, I also knew River couldn't, but I wasn't going to remind him of that when I knew deep down that he already knew.

Knocking sounded at the door, soft at first and then louder, before Justine burst into the room.

I had no time to stand from the couch to greet her before she tackle-hugged me into the cushions. "Holy shit. You're here."

"I am." I laughed. "Why are you so surprised by that?"

She sat up and moved next to me, her hands still holding on to me. "I'm the one that found your dorm empty and answered Cillian's call, then found a half-dead River stumbling down the street. River told me that you were away, and I knew he was keeping something big from me." She glanced next to me and shot him a nasty glare. "I had no clue what the hell was happening besides surmising that you were in some real shit."

I glanced over at River. He'd kept Cillian's secret, which I appreciated, but he at least could have given her some sort of story. "Didn't want to ease her worries even in the slightest?"

"I was in a mood," was all he had to say for himself.

Telling Cillian's secret wasn't something I intended to do, but seeing Justine, looking into her muddy-red eyes, and feeling the sincerity of how much she'd worried... The thought of keeping her completely out of the loop didn't sit well with me.

"There's a lot I can't tell you because they're not my secrets to share," I said, "but the world is a lot bigger than we thought and Cillian needs my help. I was taken by someone from his home, and we still need to find a way to make sure that same person can't hurt anyone else. Also, Cillian is my fated mate, but that's about all I can tell you right now."

Her jaw popped, and her lips parted slightly as she blinked at me. "I'm sorry, what? You didn't say so, but it sounds like Cillian isn't who he made us all believe he was. Like he's not a hybrid but something else."

"I really can't say." Though, we all knew by not saying I was admitting she was right. "Just know that I really appreciate everything you did to keep Cillian updated and to help River."

She lightly nudged me with her shoulder. "Of course. That mate of yours was a hot mess. I guess it makes more sense now. He didn't just have a crush on you. You two share a real connection." There was an awe in her voice, but a sadness in her eyes.

Vampires didn't have fated mates. Not unless one was an original vampire like my Aunt Amersyn. Justine would never know the soul-deep connection I had with Cillian—but also didn't really have, thanks to us never actually completing the bond.

"Secrets and mystery aside—" she squeezed my hand "—I'm glad you're okay and that you're back."

A grimace graced my face. "I'm not staying."

"And neither am I," River added.

"Am I allowed to know where the two of you plan on going?" she asked. I expected her words to be filled with hurt, but they were more curious than anything else.

"Not yet," I said, "but as soon as I can share more, you'll be among the first we tell. I promise."

She leaned forward and hugged me. "I'm not a stage-five clinger, Dawsyn. I get that there's some shit going down and the less people who know, the better, for the time being. Just know that while I'm okay giving you the space you need, I'm here if you guys need help with whatever is going on. I might not be taking protector classes like River, but that doesn't mean I haven't learned to fight."

Looking into her darkening gaze, I had no doubts about that.

"Thank you," I said. "Seriously, it means a lot."

She stood up and grinned. "You're welcome. Now, I need my afternoon fix of caffeine from Cappa's Cart. Care to join me?"

Leaving the dorm and being out more than necessary didn't feel like the right choice, so I regrettably turned her down. "While I would kill for a decent drink right now, we can't stay for much longer. I need to get back to Cillian."

Justine pulled me up and into a proper hug, something we'd never done before yet felt natural after our time apart. "Be careful."

I nodded, but River spoke first. "She has me. She'll be fine."

That wasn't the only reason I'd be fine, but he also wasn't wrong. Between having my best friend by my side and being with my mate again, I knew there was no safer place.

All too soon, I had a feeling that thought would be tested to its limits.

Chapter Two

CILLIAN

I was a fool for so many reasons, but the most current was ignoring Dawsyn to the point she'd left Drago. Without me.

Did I believe she'd return within the day as she'd promised? Sure. But I should have been with her. I should have pulled my head out of my ass long before now. Hell, it never should have been there to begin with.

I'd been letting the child in me take over. The one who wanted to pout and rage about all the stupid shit that had been going wrong for him instead of finding solutions to make things right again.

The most infuriating part was that by doing so, I was giving Knox exactly what he'd hoped for—my world in shambles.

Dawsyn was my life. I'd told myself that a week ago when I'd thought there was a chance I wouldn't ever see her again. Yet, I'd so easily let her go again. All because I didn't want to face the reality of leaving the dark hole that I'd hidden myself in.

I didn't want to face my father or my grandmother or the people of Drago that I'd let down the moment I'd chosen to take the life from Knox.

That piece of shit had vanished after I'd gone to search for Dawsyn, only then learning what I'd done. None of us had seen or sensed him since.

I stared at the wall of the cave, still in the back corner I'd claimed upon my return from Mystics Academy. The grey walls hadn't changed in the days I'd kept myself confined. The cracks were still ever present. The dirt still dry and dusty beneath me. The air still cool against my skin.

Not for the first time, I slammed my head back against the wall behind me. My frustration with myself was almost too much to handle.

I knew I needed to get up, to do something, but there wasn't an ounce of motivation inside me. Not even to find Knox.

He'd won even though I'd killed him.

He'd taken my mate bond, burned our town, killed thousands, tortured my father... All for what?

I had no idea, and I couldn't see how we were going to beat him.

"Yack!" the grandmother I'd successfully avoided the last few days said from much too close. "No wonder Dawsyn left. It smells like the devil's rotten shit back here."

"Go the fuck away," I snarled.

"That's no way to talk to your grandmother," she countered, still coming closer as if she didn't have a single bit of self-preservation left inside her.

Though, as much as I hated her in the moment, I could admit that there wasn't a possibility of me actually hurting her. Not in this scenario. Not unless I was forced to.

"You're not my grandmother," I deadpanned.

She came to stand in front of me, leaning against the wall I'd been staring at, and she crossed her arms with that annoying smirk on her face. "Over a decade of living with you and caring for you until you ventured out on your own, and I'm nothing now, huh?"

I finally raised my eyes to her face, the sneer on mine deepening by the second. "You became nothing the moment you allowed that asshole to kill the residents here and take my mate. You have no idea what I lost that day."

It hadn't just been Dawsyn and our bond. It had been my family. My uncles and Nannio. They were all I'd had, and she'd been everything to me, no matter how crazy she was. Now... She was nothing. At least, she needed to be nothing. I couldn't trust her any longer. Not with the lives of others that she'd so carelessly tossed aside to stand by Knox's side.

"I saved as many as I could," she said, this time without the ring of crazy in her voice and her eyes glossed over.

I scoffed and stood, towering over her barely five-foot

height. "Bullshit. If you think that, you're even more insane than people have always said."

She straightened slightly. "I waited to come to you and have this conversation so that you could have time to calm down, but I see you're still not capable of listening."

She turned to step away, but I grabbed her upper arm. "Let's get one thing straight. I'll never have a desire to listen to you again. No matter what my father says. He might think we need your help to finish this, but you're not my only resource any longer."

Her lips thinned. "You're talking about that witch? She has nothing on me."

"How do you know about Beatrix?" As far as I knew, Dawsyn hadn't told anyone that her grandmother was helping us, and I hadn't disclosed much either. Not even to Lykem.

The haughty look returned to her wrinkled face. "Now you want to listen?"

Did I? She very well could be tricking us all. My father seemed to believe she was still on our side, but all it took was picturing the bodies of my uncles to remember what she'd allowed to happen.

Fuck it. If I knew what information she was trying to feed everyone else, at least I could prepare for ways to counter her.

I released her arm and stepped back as far as I could get from her in the confined space. "Talk, but if you lie to me, your time here is over."

"There's my grandson," she murmured with a bit of pride I didn't expect or want. She went back to lean against the wall opposite me, leaving about six feet of space between us. Not enough, but acceptable.

"What did you come here to tell me?" I asked, since I knew there was no way she'd wanted to check on my wellbeing.

Her face softened, and her shoulders relaxed. Hell, even her pulse slowed. There were no telltale signs that she was nervous or getting ready to string a slew of lies together. My inner walls rose even higher at that.

"There's something about me that I never told you," she began. "I've always allowed people to call me the crazy dragon. In fact, it was what I wanted."

"Are you looking for a pat on the back at a job well done?" I droned.

Her lips thinned as she continued, ignoring my question. "What only your mother, father, and the elder Mantha know is that I'm not crazy at all. I see the future, Cillian. I knew what Knox was going to plan. I've known for years, and I've been trying to prepare you and everyone else for this devastation, but there were some things that even I couldn't see happening." She wiped a single tear from her cheek. "Like Jerome and Fennec."

My chest contracted, and the air became not only thicker but hotter around me. Every breath was forced as I observed her facial features, waiting for her to reveal a different truth.

Yet, watching her, seeing how calm and steady she was, how sure her words were, I felt like I had very little choice but to believe her.

Though, that didn't mean I was letting her off so easily.

"You can see the future, like a dragon seer?" I asked. As far as I'd been told, those had only existed in our early days and hadn't been seen since before Drago was created.

She nodded. "I have been since the moment I was born. When my parents realized it, they trained me not to say anything. They feared I'd be used and taken advantage of. As I grew and began to let things slip, I saw what they'd meant and paid the price heavily for that."

"What do you mean?" Fuck. I would not have sympathy for this woman right now.

She waved a hand in front of herself flippantly. "That's beside the point and not why I'm here. I don't need your pity, but I do need your trust and understanding. It's the only way we're going to win."

"Win?" I raised a brow. "My father told me that Knox was basically unbeatable now."

"No, Darius said you'd need my help to beat Knox now that you killed him, but I can see why you heard otherwise."

Yeah, working with Estelle was furthest down on the list of options I felt we currently had.

"Regardless," she continued, "I saw what Knox was going to do. I knew he was alive. I knew he had your father. And out of all the possibilities, working alongside your brother was the only way to minimize the losses."

"There were still thousands!" I roared, unable to temper the fury inside me. "Your son died, I assume at

Knox's hand. Your grandson lost his mate. Your son-in-law could die any moment. More families than you can comprehend were ripped apart. All because you didn't just tell people what you knew. Instead, you tricked them into thinking you were insane, and for what? To keep your secret? In a pathetic attempt to save a grandson you never really knew? To show everyone you're more than crazy? That you're heartless, too?"

My voice was strained and elevated, but I did my best to keep quiet. I didn't need the others to come and see what was going on.

More tears pooled in her eyes. I told myself they were for show, but as she spoke with a cracked voice, my hardened heart wavered once more.

"Jerome wasn't supposed to die," she whispered. "He was... I hadn't seen..." Her hand covered her mouth, then she looked down and away from me, seemingly trying to get her emotions under control.

I watched with scrutinizing eyes as her chest stuttered and she struggled to stop the tears from falling. "Why were Jerome and Fennec targeted?"

She glanced back at me. "I was just trying to keep you safe. Jerome was Knox's blood family, too. He could have killed Knox, given him what he wanted, but he'd refused. When Fennec was killed first, Jerome lost all hope. His mate was gone, and instead of fighting for vengeance as I'd assumed he'd do, he wanted to die, too. Before I could suggest another solution, Knox gave him that wish."

Fuck! My hand ripped through my hair, and this time it was my turn to look away.

Her sincerity was slowly killing me. I wanted to hate this woman for what she'd participated in. I wanted to blame her for everything that had gone wrong within our realm and with me for the last few years. She'd known, and from the outside, it seemed as if she'd done nothing to stop the devastation. Yet...

I couldn't look at her any longer without seeing how she'd suffered right alongside everyone else.

"I still don't understand how you working with Knox was the best solution," I said with less anger. "The amount of destruction is unfathomable."

She wiped the last of the tears from her frail cheeks. "And it could have been worse."

"How so?"

"As a seer, I don't just see one future, but I get glimpses of the outcomes to certain decisions," she answered solemnly. "It was either this or our whole world would have burned. Knox was ready to die alongside all of us. He was going to burn Drago to ash, but I found him, earned his trust, and showed him another option."

My jaw tensed at the thought of her other option. "And what was that?"

"That he could take everything from the family who had abandoned him." Her eyes were hard. "Knox was raised to believe that his mother killed him. Left him for dead in that dark forest all because your father didn't want to raise another man's child, but that isn't even close to what happened. Though, convincing your brother of that was never going to happen. I had to play into his hand. I had to show him a different path to vengeance. One that would allow you to stop him."

"Except I didn't," I said tersely. "I only made him more powerful, because you never told me what I needed to know."

"I told you what I could, and you did exactly what you were supposed to," she replied. "Your father might have made it seem like all hope is lost, but our fight is far from over. You will stop this war, Cillian. I've seen that from the very beginning, and I've never lied to you. I may have ignored you to avoid doing so, and you can disagree with my choices all you want, but this was our only option that allowed even some of us to live."

"How am I going to stop Knox?" I asked, hating that it was because of the grandmother I wanted to forget that I was finally finding my purpose again.

"You're going to use the syphon spell I told you to find, and your mate is going to help you," she said. "You only need the potion, not the witch. Get that and we'll end this as a family. Just like I foresaw."

Family.

The word no longer held the same emotions for me that it once did. Though, there was one person who meant more to me than family, and I needed to find and apologize to her immediately.

Chapter Three

DAWSYN

Pushing River through the portal was a highlight to my day that I hadn't known I needed.

"What the fuck, D?" he sputtered as he fell to his knees, no longer in the frigid mountains, but in the sweltering land of Drago.

His back arched as he took a deep inhale, and I smirked. "Not what you expected?"

He glared up at me as he got to his feet. "Considering I didn't expect you to push me while cackling just like GiGi, I'd say no."

I tossed an arm around his waist once he was up. "It was all in good fun. At least you didn't have time to overthink anything."

That didn't seem to help his demeanor. Neither did looking out toward the city that was crumbling. "Shit. That's worse than I imagined, even after what you told me."

The smoke had stopped since the attacks ceased, but that didn't mean the destruction wasn't still present.

Half-toppled buildings barely stood just a few miles ahead of us. Leveled houses appeared beside them along with scorched trees and dead land. It was all heartbreaking, even though this wasn't our home.

Though, the more days that passed, the more I wondered if this would one day be the place I woke up in every day.

That's not something we need to focus on yet, my wolf said. *We need to go check on our mate.*

She'd been firmly against me leaving Drago, but I hadn't been helping Cillian with his shitty mood. He had to find it in himself to either find the will to fight back or...not.

I'd only been gone a few hours, but I hoped that had made a difference for him. In a positive way.

Not only did his people need that, but I did as well.

I needed my mate. I needed him to want to fight for the bond we'd lost and everything that we could still have.

"Ready to run?" I asked River with a wicked grin.

"Run or *race*?"

I was already stepping away from him. He knew the answer and I had no qualms about stealing a head start.

When we were little, racing was our favorite pastime. There were never any prizes. Just ultimate bragging rights, which I still held.

Just as I began to shift, he yelled, "Cheater."

There were no rules in our races. Just smarter choices

that he didn't usually think to make.

His reflexes seemed faster than I remembered, though. It had been well over a year since we'd raced each other, and my best friend was no longer the scrawny beanpole he was as a teenager.

His ruddy wolf appeared on my left, and I snarked at my own. *Where's the glow when we need it?*

Do we really need it? she countered.

Bragging rights aren't meant to be lost.

I could sense her internal sigh, but she took a deep inhale. Upon exhaling, the extra surge of energy I'd started to get used to pushed through us. Though, not as swiftly as it had been just a few days before.

River's wolf snarled as the distance between us increased, but surprisingly, he didn't fall as far behind as I expected.

Our wolves ran at breakneck speeds, dodging trees and keeping an eye out for anything that didn't belong. Just because I wanted to have a bit of fun with my friend didn't mean I'd forgotten that Drago was still a literal warzone.

I doubted that Knox had acted in the hours I'd been gone, but nothing was impossible.

All too soon, we were skidding to a stop at the mouth of the cave, dust swirling up around us.

Before I could shift, River's wolf pounced on mine and playfully bit at my neck just like old times. My heart wanted to soar with the nostalgia of the act, but there was a piece of it missing, preventing me from really immersing myself into the moment.

River seemed to catch on quickly to it, too.

We both shifted back, and before I could look over at him, he was at my side and wrapping his arms around me. "Everything is going to be okay, D."

I nodded against his shoulder. "I know. Doesn't mean that it's easy to take in the meantime, though."

He released me, then nudged my chin with his thumb. "That's what I'm here for now."

"Even though you can't win a race, you are a rather excellent best friend," I teased.

His brows furrowed. "Speaking of, that was dirty using your new juju to win. I would have had you otherwise, regardless of your cheating head start."

I knew he wasn't wrong, but I wasn't going to tell him that. His ego seemed big enough already.

"Tell yourself whatever you need to in order to feel better." I patted his chest and turned to head inside the caves to find Cillian.

The drive to touch him and make sure he was okay was growing stronger by the second, and it hadn't even been half a day since I'd left his side.

Fuck our broken bond, I thought, the words tinged with malice. The more hours that passed without the tether to Cillian reigniting, the more furious I became with fate. I didn't know if this was the doing of the Moon Goddess or something greater to do with dragons, but either way, the path I'd been set on was fucked.

My thoughts were constantly torn between wishing for the connection I'd once had and hoping it didn't return so that we could prove the bond was nothing more than a joke.

The need and feelings and want I'd maintained for Cillian even when I tied to Knox had remained all-consuming. So, what was the point of the bond? What were we missing?

At the moment, I didn't think anything. Yet, I was still resentful at its absence.

It was a tug-a-war of emotions I seemed to only keep under wraps when I had my mate with me.

Just as I stepped through the threshold of the cave, his crisp, earthy scent hit me right in the chest.

My head snapped up, and I searched in front of me, knowing he was there but unable to see far enough into the darkness of the tunnels.

I stayed anchored in place, unsure of what I was going to see once my mate came closer. Was he angry with me for leaving? Was he trying to escape the cave, running from his problems? Running toward me?

River stood just a foot behind me, but as the rumble of my mate sounded from the shadows in front of us, my best friend took another step back. "I'm going to go...walk."

"Not too far," I said without looking back.

Just a second after I heard River's retreating steps, Cillian's face came into view. His jaw was tight, but his eyes were bright. A first in what felt like much too long.

I started to ask what was going on, but his hands were on me in the next second, one tangling in my hair, the other gripping my jaw and neck.

Our mouths collided like fireworks, and my fingers latched onto his shirt, bunching the fabric as I pushed up onto my toes.

He held me tightly and kissed the hell out of me until my stomach filled with a need that spread throughout the rest of my body. The sultry taste of him and the vibrations from his chest had me clawing at his body and forgetting where we were or what I had been worried about just two seconds before.

As I struggled to breathe, his hands trailed lower on my body until he gripped my ass and lifted me up so that I could wrap my legs around his waist.

There was a fleeting thought that told me to stop what was happening, to figure out what had brought this version of Cillian back to me, but I swatted it away without thinking twice.

Selfishly, I let him devour me, not only because it seemed like this was what he needed, but because I fucking needed *him*.

I needed to feel this connection between us, to know that there was still a simmering passion there that grew by the second and that we couldn't ignore, even if we wanted to.

My heels dug into his back, and I grabbed his hair as a rumble rolled through me. The need to bite him, to mark him as mine, was so fucking strong in that moment.

I pulled out of the kiss only to move my lips down his jaw, then to his neck. My canines elongated, my mouth salivating as his pulse pounded beneath my lips.

Mine. All fucking mine.

"I'm so sorry, Dawsyn," Cillian's tortured words cut through my thoughts like water on flames.

Suddenly, it wasn't just his arousal that I could sense, but it was his pain. Jagged edges that needed to be soothed and healed.

With a little regret, I reined in my need and the animalistic half of me so that I could be the mate Cillian needed me to be.

"You have nothing to be sorry for," I said and had several other things to add, but he cut me off.

His thumbs brushed over my cheeks. "Yes, I do. I let the grief win. I wasn't strong for you when you needed me to be. I made mistakes and..."

"And nothing," I said, still clinging to him. "What matters now is what you're going to do next. What happened before can't be changed. We can't bring back the dead. We can't change our past actions. All we can do is make better choices and forge ahead."

His eyes briefly shifted to the cave entrance, then back to me. "Estelle came to me."

That fucking bitch.

I'd threatened her before I'd gone back to Earth. Told her if she didn't give Cillian the space that he needed to process the shitshow she helped cause that I'd rip her throat out, which I should have done back when I'd escaped the cell.

"I'm sorry, Cillian," I said. "I should have never left."

He shook his head, and the sadness I expected to see in his eyes never came. In fact, he seemed...I didn't know, but more than his sudden show of need for me, something had changed for my mate.

Maybe your idea of giving him space hadn't been all that crazy, my wolf admitted.

"You did exactly what you should have," he said. "And I'm going to start doing the same. I had so much hurt inside me that I began to question everything, wondering how I could have let all this happen, but I never had a choice. None of us did."

"What do you mean?" I asked.

His hands moved to my back, holding me tighter against him. "My grandmother... She's not insane. She's a dragon seer."

I blinked several times. "What now?"

"She saw what was going to happen with Knox."

I tried to process how that was possible and why the fuck she would have chosen to work with him, but the annoying part of my brain that allowed the alpha in me to be diplomatic wondered if, because of what she saw, she knew there were no other options.

Just like I had when I bonded myself to that fucker.

With an annoyed sigh, I knew that was where this was headed and hated that I couldn't just hate her for what she'd done. Not when I could so easily relate.

"What did she see before, and what does she presume is going to happen now?" I asked.

"It's not just about what she sees," he said. "It's more than that. She saw the outcome of various scenarios, and there is only one possible way to beat Knox. One that she's been trying to lead us to this whole time. She could have stopped me from killing him, but she didn't. It was a choice I had to make in order for us to win."

That made me wonder if being a seer and what Brixley could do were actually totally different things. Brixley had warned me of my chosen mate, but she hadn't seemed to know anything about the consequences to any of my choices.

"So, now that you know that, things are better between the two of you?" I asked, hoping for Cillian that was true, even if I still didn't really care for the woman, regardless of what I'd just learned.

His lips thinned. "I don't know. They're different, and I don't think they can go back to the way they were, but that's the least of my worries right now."

That last bit was said with a delicious growl and had my legs tightening around his waist even more.

"We need to meet with my father and Estelle," he said, and the fire that had started to flicker within my core fizzled out again. At least until he lightly kissed me again. "I've missed you, Dawsyn. More than you can fucking imagine."

"Oh, I can imagine." Hell, I was living the same feelings, but I wasn't going to rub that in his face when I was finally seeing the Cillian I'd first met come through again. "But none of that matters. We'll get through this together."

His nose ran up my neck, sending shivers down my spine. "We will. I promise."

And I fucking believed him.

Chapter Four

CILLIAN

A fog had been lifted from my mind. I'd been so focused on what had gone wrong and what I'd felt were my failures that I couldn't see all the good I had right in front of me. All that I still had to fight for.

Dawsyn was everything I needed. I'd known that for some time, yet I'd let my darker thoughts convince me otherwise and continued to put things of less importance in front of her.

Holding her in my arms and apologizing didn't seem like enough, but I'd do that every day for the rest of my life until I felt like it was.

"I should probably find River," she said. "Feels rude to bring him to a warzone and then ditch him."

"I'm surprised you brought him here at all." Last I'd heard, Dawsyn had wanted her best friend to stay as far from this fight as possible.

She shrugged and wiggled out of my arms. "I had to consider if the roles were reversed, what would I want? It was too soon to have him join us before, but this feels right now. Having us all together."

I nodded and lowered my head, pressing our foreheads together. "I agree. I'm sorry I didn't go with you back to Earth."

"I think it was just the thing we both needed."

I raised a brow. "Both needed? Is everything okay?"

She smirked and pressed her palm over my chest. "I mean this in the most loving way, but if you were still in your daze when I returned, I was going to drag you out of that cave by your hair and dunk you in that freezing water we used to clean up in before."

I chuckled and grinned. "I would have loved to see you try."

"I still can," she challenged.

Oh, I had no doubts she'd enjoy that a little too much.

"How about we go find River so we can go meet with my father?" I suggested. "I've been ignoring things for too long now. It's time to make our next move and figure out what Knox might be doing in the meantime."

"Your dad hasn't been out of his bed, but he seems to be doing better," she said. "Staying awake longer and eating more with each meal. Though, still physically weak."

A rumble rolled through my chest as I turned us in the direction River had wandered. "I hate that he'd suffered for so long and none of us had known. Even more, I hate that I'd assumed he'd chosen to leave, getting himself killed because he couldn't handle my mother's death. Instead, he'd been taken against his will and none of us had truly looked for him."

What really bothered me was why he hadn't reached out. Had Knox threatened more lives if my father told me where he was? We should have been able to mind link, even now, yet I hadn't heard his voice in my head since I was a child.

I shoved those thoughts aside and wrapped an arm around Dawsyn. Her body heat soaked into me, allowing my chest to expand, and I stood a little taller just having her at my side.

I'd spent too many days worrying and not enough of them claiming the life I wanted.

That was ending now. I would fight for what was mine and that was Dawsyn. I couldn't stop just because I physically had her. There was still so much at stake that I wasn't willing to give up on. I just needed to continue reminding myself of that.

She leaned her head against my arm, a small smile playing on her lips. Neither of us said anything more. We soaked in each other's company, and that was enough.

River hadn't ventured far. Probably just far enough that he wasn't eavesdropping on our conversation, which made my respect for him grow a bit more.

I stepped forward first and shook his hand. "Thanks for coming."

He gestured lightly to Dawsyn. "I'd have been here sooner if it wasn't for her."

In that, I had no doubt.

"You're here now," she drawled. "Keep complaining and you'll see how far that gets you."

River didn't seem bothered by her threat. Instead, he refocused on me. "What do you need?"

I hadn't given him enough credit before. I knew he was attending Mystics Academy to become one of the supernatural guards or whatever they called them, but just because someone had a desire to do something didn't mean they should.

Though, looking at River, seeing the drive in his eyes, the steady rise and fall of his chest, and the strong stance he kept as his gaze continued to sweep around us, watching for danger, I knew that wasn't the case for this wolf shifter.

"We need to meet with my father and grandmother," I said. "They were both with Knox and know more than we do of his plans. At least, that's the hope. Once we can gather what they know, then we'll resume the hunt for the syphon spell."

River glanced at Dawsyn. "The thing you asked GiGi to help with?"

She nodded. "She has everything but one ingredient." Then, she looked up at me. "I thought we might not need that spell, though?"

"I didn't think we would once we knew who we were dealing with, but after learning Knox is an Ember dragon and talking to my grandmother, we still do," I said.

Ember dragons were the rarest of our kind. They were more of a genetic defect than they were anything else. You couldn't breed and grow a clan of powerful shifters. It was pure luck when one was born.

Or in our case, disastrous fucking luck.

Being an Ember meant that Knox was essentially like a phoenix who could continue rising from the ashes. I still didn't know how my killing him made him more powerful, but that was what I hoped to learn soon enough.

"Well, let's go figure all that out," River said. "I'm sure I can manage to fill in the pieces on my own to keep up with the conversations."

He began walking past us and toward the cave entrance, making Dawsyn grin. "He's grown up a lot more than I'd given him credit for."

"I heard that," he called back, but kept walking.

My lips pressed to the top of Dawsyn's head. "I'm sure the both of you have."

We followed behind River, catching up to him at the opening.

"It's dark inside, but there are torches along the walls to give just enough light," Dawsyn warned him.

He smirked. "Learning to be one of the community protectors isn't just about book smarts. Do you have any idea how many times I've been locked in a pitch-black room until I could train my eyes to see what they shouldn't be able to?"

Her shoulders drooped slightly. "No, but now I feel like I've been missing out on some shit."

"Maybe you should have enrolled in a few classes like

I told you to do," he quipped just before giving her his back and walking forward.

Dawsyn quickly bent down and picked up a rock, throwing it at River's head before he could completely disappear into the shadows. "Maybe you should kiss my ass."

I laughed at their antics, but only briefly. "As entertaining as this is, we need to hurry. I told Estelle that I would find you and then meet her in my father's room."

She straightened within an instant. "Do we need to get anyone else?"

I shook my head. "This is a family matter. For now. Not everyone needs to know about all the things that might be discussed during this first conversation. I'm sure Estelle has passed along what was necessary before now."

Her stare softened, but there was still an underlying concern there that I assumed was for me.

"I'm okay now," I promised. "I won't let emotion take over again."

She squeezed my hand as we continued walking, catching up with River. "There's nothing wrong with emotions. They're healthy. Just don't shut me out again and I'll let you keep all your body parts intact."

Her grin was wicked but appreciated.

"Noted."

I took the lead after that. Even though I hadn't been to my father's room yet, thanks to my own idiocy, Estelle had told me where they were keeping him.

Not calling her Nannio after a lifetime of only

thinking of my grandmother as that was confusing. Not only to my brain, but my heart. I still wanted to be angry with her for keeping the secrets she did, but the more time that passed since our conversation, the more I was able to understand her reasoning. As asinine as it was, being able to see the future seemed like more of a curse than a blessing.

A burden she was forced to handle as best she could.

Did I believe she had to do so alone? Initially, no. Yet, I couldn't get it out of my head the added benefit she had of seeing other scenarios play out based on certain decisions. If she knew by telling someone just one thing that the outcome would never come to fruition...

Yeah, that was fucking terrible. For all involved. Especially my uncles. She hadn't been able to save them, and while I'd initially thought she hadn't given a shit that her son and his mate had died, I couldn't deny the grief I'd felt coursing off her as she spoke of those moments when everything had gone wrong.

Nothing else could, though. We needed a win. Several of them. And I was going to make sure nothing stopped us from getting what we needed. Not again.

Two sections away from the kitchen and a few lefts, then a right, we'd arrived at my father's corner. He actually had a space to himself. Not one blocked out by sheets, but a small room with two torches on the walls and a blanket over the doorway.

He was sitting up on an actual mattress— something else I hadn't seen inside these caves—and his eyes looked alert, but his body was still skin and bones. Though, the bruising I'd glimpsed before had at least faded.

"Son."

With the single word, my heart felt as if a knife was being twisted through the middle of it. For years, I yearned to hear my father's voice again. Yet, having him right in front of me, knowing he was alive... I was still conflicted between wrapping my arms around him like the child I'd once been and keeping my distance, knowing there would be no chance of getting those moments back that we'd lost.

"I'm sorry I couldn't get here sooner," I said, standing at the base of his bed.

"None of that matters much now," Estelle said. "We're together, and we have the information we need. Grab a chair and let's talk."

The soft tone of her words wasn't one I was used to from her, but I didn't let that impact me the way it would have before I learned she was working with Knox.

As Dawsyn took her seat between me and River, she pointed to her best friend. "This is River. He's been part of my family—"

"Since you were born and you trust him explicitly," Estelle finished for her. "If I didn't already know who he was, he wouldn't be here."

There was the snark I was used to.

Thankfully, Dawsyn had a crazy grandmother herself, and she didn't seem fazed.

Once we were all seated around my father, I glanced

at Estelle. "How long do we have before Knox resurfaces?"

She glanced between the four of us. "Five moon cycles beginning the moment you killed him, and you've already wasted two of them."

Dawsyn snarled. "Maybe if you hadn't abandoned him for a brother that he knew nothing about, he wouldn't have needed those two days to wrap his head around all this shit.

Estelle's eyes darkened. "Watch it, Wolf. I might be old, but that doesn't make me incapable of defending myself with more than words."

This time, it was my turn to snarl. "Enough. Dawsyn has every right to feel the way she does, regardless of your reasons for not telling us what you were doing. You won't threaten her again or we both walk away."

My grandmother stared me down, unblinking and silent. I wondered briefly if right then she was seeing a future based on a choice I absolutely would make, but she didn't give any indication of whether my thoughts were true.

"Fine," she said. "Let's stick to the facts, then. We have three days left to stop Knox before he reaches his full power. Within that timeframe, you need to complete the syphon spell and you need to get real comfortable with a knife."

"Why?" I asked.

"Because you'll have to obliterate Knox's heart with a particular blade if you don't want him to come back to life again."

Chapter Five

DAWSYN

I wanted to choke the life from Estelle. Cillian had already lost enough, so I wouldn't follow through on that urge, but he didn't need someone toxic in his life. Regardless of this convenient ability she seemed to have with seeing the future, I was finding it hard to maintain my alpha persona and understand the position she'd been in. Especially when those actions hurt my mate.

"How do you know we only have three days left?" I asked. "Is that something he freely shared with you or something you already knew?"

Estelle kept a straight face and a neutral voice. "Neither. It's something I saw. We need to be prepared to fight by the fifth night or Knox will be reborn. And thanks to Cillian being the one to kill him last, Knox will inherit his true Ember powers.

I had no idea what that meant, but Cillian explained for the rest of us. "He'll be able to burn Drago to its core."

Estelle nodded. "Within days of waking and with little effort, Knox will be able to sink his hands into the earth and send fire through the ground that will crumble everything around us, consuming every soul still here."

"And with the syphon spell, we'll be able to take that power from him?" River asked, giving me an idea.

"Essentially, but it won't kill him to lose his power," she said. "Cillian will still need to do that with the dagger I will give him once he has the syphon spell."

"And after knowing you were working with him, why should we trust you?" River asked next. "You say you were only there because you had to be, but what reassurances do we have that you're not only here because Knox asked you to be?"

"These are questions I find acceptable."

Estelle didn't need to glance my way for me to know that she was trying to poke at me, but I wasn't going to bite. This time.

"You don't," she added. "You'll just have to decide for yourself whether to trust me or not, but I assure you, without my help, you won't win. And what you lose will be more than you can fathom. Knox's destruction won't stop with our world. It will undoubtedly filter to Earth."

"Enough with the threats," Darius said, then coughed several times. "There can't be any other questioning of loyalties or past decisions. What's done is done, and all we can do now is work toward finishing this as quickly as possible." He glanced at his son longingly. "You were never supposed to be part of this. I'm sorry I couldn't stop things before they got so far."

Cillian tensed next to me. "Why didn't you tell any of us what happened? You could have reached out to me before it was too late."

"I was a stubborn man, and it cost me dearly." The wrinkles around Darius's face deepened as his pale grey eyes peered at me, then back at Cillian. "Don't make my same mistakes." He coughed again. "I thought I could fix this myself, but I didn't know what I do now. I told no one that I'd gone to the forest that day. Nobody knew your mother had another son, and I wanted to keep it that way, but I only succeeded in one task that day."

"And what was that?" Cillian asked as I tried to remain a steady presence for him at his side.

"I killed Knox's father." A darkness flashed over Darius's eyes. "I know I just said that the past doesn't matter, but there are a few things you should know. We didn't abandon Knox. He lived with us the first three months of his life, then Nivon showed up."

Darius closed his eyes and took a shaky breath before continuing. "He wanted both his son and Maribelle, but I was already mated to your mother. She refused to go with him or give up her son. Nivon argued at first and then had a change of heart, agreeing to our compromise. He could still be a part of Knox's life, but Maribelle and I would be the child's parents. Eventually, he seemed to take this well, but we should have known better. He'd asked to hold his son just once and then he promised to leave us be. As soon as Maribelle handed Knox over, Nivon snapped his neck, telling us that if he couldn't have him, then neither could we."

My hand covered my mouth as I tried to hold in my gasp. What a fucking monster.

"Your mother reached for the baby, but Nivon wouldn't even give us the benefit of allowing us to bury our child," Darius added. "We had no clue Knox had come back to life or what he was before dying that first time. He hadn't been old enough to wear the mark of the flame."

"But Knox was raised by his father," Cillian pointed out.

Darius nodded weakly. "He was until I showed up almost twenty years ago and killed him. After your mother died, it was my intention to go there and get the justice she deserved. While I did that, I also learned Knox hadn't been killed that day."

Cillian leaned forward in his chair. "What do you mean, 'justice' for Mom? Did Nivon return to kill her? I thought her death was some unknown event."

"That's what I told everyone," Estelle said. "I saw what would happen for the first time then. Nobody could know Knox existed yet."

My mate stiffened and turned his head slowly toward his grandmother. "You knew how she died and that my father was there the whole time?"

"I did, and none of us could have done anything about it then or we wouldn't be here to have this conversation."

Fuck. I hated so much for Cillian that she possibly had a point. Though, we had no way to be sure of that other than trusting her word to be true, which was a hell of a lot harder for me to do than I assumed it was for Cillian.

"Regardless of all that," Darius continued, "Nivon died, but Knox was already grown by then, and he took me by surprise. Before I could understand what was happening, he'd knocked me out and taken me to those tunnels. When I woke back up, my energy was a quarter of what it had been, and my ability to communicate with the mind link was gone. Even now, I can't use it. I have no idea what Knox did to me."

Cillian took a harsh exhale as I reached for his hand. "But you're alive, and we're going to get you better," I said, reminding everyone that while this story fucking sucked, not all was lost. Cillian had regained a parent, and we still had three days to make things right where Knox was concerned. We could work with that.

While I was glad for my mate that he had answers to questions I was sure he'd had for many years, this conversation wasn't going to help us with our limited time.

The idea I'd had earlier resurfaced, and I used that as an opportunity to change the subject to more productive topics. "There's an issue with the spell and an ingredient not actually existing any longer. But I have a family member who is the supernatural version of a syphon. Could that work instead of the spell?"

Bringing in my family hadn't originally been something I wanted to do, but if it was either that or watching this world burn, I knew I didn't have a choice.

Plus, I knew my aunt would help. All of them would if only I asked. Hell, possibly even if I didn't.

Estelle was already shaking her head. "She would die from the energy she'd have to consume. We need to fight the kind of magic Knox contains only with the spell I sent Cillian in search of."

I hadn't said I was referencing a woman, yet Estelle knew to say "she". Maybe she really could see multiple futures...

I believe she can, my wolf said. *I like her even less than you, but her heart seems to be in the right place, even if her attitude isn't.*

Great. Knowing that was a lot harder than hating her.

"So, we know what Knox is capable of, but why?" River asked. "Why would he want to destroy this world and not just take it over?"

"Knox was told his whole life that his mother and I had abandoned him. Left him for dead, essentially," Darius spoke again. "That he was an abomination nobody would understand. His father was trying to turn him into a weapon to take over, but nobody knew what Estelle did. Nobody knew that it wasn't just Knox dying that would trigger his ultimate power, yet Nivon killed him every other week for over a decade."

My stomach churned with sympathy. Knox didn't deserve a single shred of kind emotion after all he'd done, yet...that was exactly what he had from every single person in this room the moment Darius spoke those words.

Even Cillian's shoulders softened as he asked his next question. "Did you tell Knox the truth when he had you?"

Darius nodded. "He never believed me, though."

"But he heard you," I said. "Even if he didn't consciously accept your truth, he heard you, and that could make all the difference in the end."

Estelle raised a greying brow at me. "Are you suggesting that we try to merely *talk* Knox out of moving forward with his plans?"

"Abso-fucking-lutely not," I replied. "If killing him is the only way to ensure the madness is dealt with, then he needs to die. What I think will help is how easily he will go down. If his dragon knows the truth, then that will go a long way in minimizing the mayhem they could cause."

"I agree," River said from next to me. "I've seen it happen several times when going out during training. If the inner animal doesn't agree with the human half, they're always easier to catch, but if they're completely rogue, then it's a bloodbath. If Knox kept Darius alive all these years, then deep down, he knows he doesn't deserve to die."

"While I wish I could believe that," Cillian started, "Knox used my father to gain more power. Him being alive was not a kindness. Death would have been."

Twenty years being locked in the darkness... My mate made a valid point.

"Either way, we know what we're dealing with now," Estelle said. "The three of you need to return to Earth and finish that spell."

It was my turn to raise a brow at her. "Any hints as to where we should start looking for something that doesn't exist?"

Her lips thinned. "I'm not a magic crystal. If I knew, I would have already told you."

"But you see us succeeding still?" Cillian asked.

She held his stare but didn't answer. "You really should be going now. I'll take care of your father."

Something told me I wasn't sure we should believe her, but at least others like Lykem and the healer Winter were here to look after him.

I glanced over at River. "I'll show you around the cave." Then, I turned to Cillian. "Finish talking to your father. We'll meet you out front when you're ready."

He may not have shown a lot of emotion when he walked in the room, but Darius didn't look well, and I didn't want Cillian to later regret not using this second chance. Did I assume his father was going to be okay? Yes, but that didn't mean shit couldn't go sideways while we were gone.

When I stood, so did Cillian, and I watched Estelle sneak out of the room behind us without another word. At least she could take a social cue.

"You don't need to go," he said softly.

"I know." My hand cupped his cheek. "I won't be far."

"Thank you," he murmured, but it wasn't necessary.

I walked out of the small space with River right behind me. Just as I turned the corner, though, Darius's strangled voice called my name.

When I peeked back around, his arms were wrapped around his waist. "Thank you for coming back for me. I understand you didn't know who I was, and yet you'd still promised to come back. That shows a true alpha."

I didn't know who he'd been talking to or how he knew so much already, but I merely smiled in return. "I'm just glad we weren't too late."

River stayed quiet beside me, and before I could decide what to show him first inside the caves, I caught a flash of white hair headed left in the next tunnel.

I grabbed River's hand and pulled him behind me. "We need to catch that dragon."

"Uh, sure." He chuckled behind me.

I felt certain that I'd just seen Winter. She'd saved Lykem's life and, given how quickly she'd healed his wounds, I wanted to know why Darius still looked like death. Not only for my curiosity, but for Cillian's heart.

"Winter," I said sharply when we turned the corner, and I couldn't see her any longer.

"Yes?" she answered without reappearing.

"It's Dawsyn. Can you come back this way?" I asked, not really wanting to chase her too deep into the cave tunnels that I wasn't all that familiar with.

I blinked, then she was standing before me. "How can I help you, Dawsyn?"

I stepped back and shook my head. "First, you can walk louder. Secondly, have you been to see Darius?"

Her mouth downturned. "I have."

"And why isn't he up and walking yet?" I pressed.

"Because he refused my help," she said softly. "I

brought him medicine, but he said his dragon would take care of what needed doing."

Interesting and slightly disturbing. Why wouldn't Darius want to get better quicker? Why suffer longer than necessary?

I didn't know, but that wasn't my problem right now. Finding the last ingredient for the syphon potion was.

"Thanks, Winter," I said. "Maybe try again if you're not too busy?"

She nodded, glancing behind me at River and no longer meeting my eyes. "Sure, Dawsyn."

I turned around and River wasn't even looking at her, which was odd because Winter was beautiful. Then again, River wasn't here for fun, and he wasn't the same boy I'd grown up with.

With my best friend in tow, we headed toward the kitchen, but I could hear too many voices in there and decided it was best if we just went out front to wait for Cillian. I wasn't sure how welcoming the other clan members would be with two wolf shifters here.

I was Cillian's mate, even if it wasn't official, but River wasn't anything to anyone here. I couldn't risk someone causing trouble we really didn't need.

As soon as we were outside, I took a deep breath and sighed. "The caves aren't all that exciting."

"No, and it's hard to tell who's coming and going from where," he added.

I poked at his chest as his eyes continued to watch

our surroundings. "You're taking this protector thing quite seriously."

"Would you rather have me pretend everything is fine after all you've told me and that I've seen?" he countered with a tilt of his head.

"Nope," I said. "I was just surprised you didn't even give Winter a second look back there."

His brow furrowed as he glanced back at the cave. "I'm not here for a fling, and she isn't my fated mate. Better that I don't."

I leaned against the cool rocks behind me and grinned. "When did you get so grown up?"

"I might be younger in physical years, but—" he tapped the side of his head, "—I'm much wiser than you up here."

My leg swung out, striking him in the shin. "I'll kick your ass anytime, Pierce."

"I'll be waiting, Chase."

Chapter Six

CILLIAN

I hadn't been alone with my father in twenty years. I'd expected to feel something deeper at the reunion, yet there was a distance between us that I wasn't sure how to get past. Neither of us knew the other anymore. I wasn't the child he left behind. Far from it.

Though, I wanted to try for both our sakes.

I took the seat Estelle had vacated and sat closer to the side of his bed. "Why aren't you better yet?"

"How much do you trust these people?" he asked, glancing toward the doorway.

"Enough that I would fight for their lives."

He coughed again, sending a couple drops of blood onto his blanket. "Because they're good people or because you are?"

"Both," I answered without hesitating. "Why?"

"The healer girl," he said quietly. "She's not a normal dragon."

This was news to me. "What do you mean?"

"I don't know," he replied. "But her energy isn't right."

"She saved Lykem, Dad. He should have died with the wounds he had. I don't think Winter is out to hurt anyone."

He licked his dry and cracked lips. "Doesn't mean she's good."

"Just because she may be different doesn't mean she's bad, either," I retorted. "I don't know Winter well, but she was born here, and I've never sensed anything off about her. What about her energy didn't you like?"

"Enough about that," he said with a rough shake of his head. "Tell me about you. I didn't expect you to have a wolf shifter mate."

His abrupt change in subject had my fingers drumming over my thighs, but since I was on limited time, I let him have his way.

"Neither did I," I said. "I met her while I was looking for the syphon spell. She and her family have been helpful throughout all this."

"I'm glad to hear it," he wheezed, trying to...do something.

"Hell, Dad. You're going to fall over." My hands shot out and righted his wobbly form. "Just let Winter help you. I can go get—"

He cut me off. "You have other things to do. Don't worry about me. I'm just glad to see you all grown up. I wish I hadn't..." Cough. Cough. Cough. "Missed so much. There wasn't a day that passed when I didn't think of you and try to reach out."

"It's okay," I said. "I understand now."

He nodded and started to lean again. "I'm going to rest. You should get going."

I helped him onto his pillow, then stood. His eyes were already closed while his chest rose and fell slowly. I lifted the blanket at his waist and covered him up before leaving the room.

Knowing he hadn't left me on purpose helped ease some of my past hurt, but something was still off and I wasn't sure it had anything to do with Winter.

My father was held captive and tortured for twenty years, though. I had to remember that. Nobody would come out of a situation like that without a few mental issues. Maybe when we returned from Earth, he'd be more...something. I didn't really know what his normal was. Too much time had passed.

I hurried through the tunnels and toward the front of the caves. When I arrived, Dawsyn and River were facing off, but they wore matching smiles.

What I wouldn't have given to have had a normal childhood.

Lykem might be my oldest friend, but I didn't have a relationship with him like these two had. I'd been too unwilling to get close to anyone other than Nannio and my uncles. It was a protection mechanism that I was suddenly realizing seemed to be more harmful than helpful, encouraging me to keep people at arm's length.

I wasn't standing there more than two seconds before Dawsyn's eyes landed on me. "Everything go okay?"

Even without the bond, she was overly attuned to

me. That thought had me wanting to complete at least a chosen mate connection with her immediately, but it never seemed like we had more than a fleeting moment to ourselves.

Soon, I'd have her all to myself, and I wasn't going to tell her no again.

I'd claim my mate just as swiftly as she'd have me.

I nodded once. "Ready to head out?"

River's eyes roamed over the sky. "And here I thought I'd be fighting a dragon or two before I left."

"Did we scare you off so easily?" Lykem's voice sounded from behind me.

His hand grasped my shoulder, and I looked over at him. Our stares met, but he didn't ask me a single thing. Just winked, then released me before heading over to River to introduce himself, but Dawsyn beat him to it.

"Riv, this is Dragon Boy," she said. "He thinks he's funnier than everyone else does."

Lykem leaned closer to River and grinned. "And the *Alpha* Wolf Girl is afraid of heights. Who would have guessed."

River held his hand up. "Me. I absolutely would have."

Dawsyn paid them no further attention as she came over to me where I was still waiting by the cave entrance. "Are you sure you're ready to leave?"

I gave her my full attention and slid my hands lightly over her arms. "I am. I'm done with whatever had a hold on me before."

"It was grief, and there was nothing wrong with it," she said softly.

"Poorly timed at a minimum, but that's beside the point." I tucked my mate into my side and glanced over at Lykem. "We'll be back within a few days, hopefully. According to Estelle, there shouldn't be any problems while we're gone, but keep up with guard rotations just in case."

"Can we trust her?" he asked, and I hesitated in my answer.

It was a valid question, and while none of my internal warnings were going off, I still didn't want to say yes.

"Enough that she can stay, but not enough that we let our guards down," I finally replied.

Estelle had been playing this game for too long. Although she was trying to protect the future, there was no way to know what kind of effects her time with Knox had on her loyalties. Hell, she might not even understand what she wants at this point.

Not only was my grandmother old as dirt, but she'd played crazy long enough that we had to consider the possibility that she just might be insane.

I at least felt confident that she wasn't going to intentionally harm anyone here. The regret she'd shown over Uncle Jerome's death was too sincere to believe otherwise.

With a few last reminders to Lykem, I led Dawsyn and River toward a clearing big enough for me to shift, which wasn't as far as it had once been.

Knox had seen to that when he'd launched more

firebombs this way at the start of the fight. Trees had burned, and fissures had formed in the mountain, but from what I had seen in my brief time walking around, the caves had stayed intact.

"Want to ride my mate?" Dawsyn said with a waggle of her brows to River.

He choked on air, sputtering and coughing. "Um, I prefer the female variety, but thanks for the offer." Then, he glanced at me. "No offense, Cillian."

"None taken."

All the while, Dawsyn cackled to herself, finding her joke funnier than the two of us had.

I shifted into my dragon form without warning and didn't miss the way River jumped back.

"Holy fuck," he muttered. "I wasn't prepared for that."

"I thought you were ready to fight some fire-breathing beasts?" Dawsyn jeered lightly.

He relaxed his body and stepped closer to me, ignoring my mate. His eyes appraised me, and he grinned. "It would be great if you could reveal yourself back home. You'd make the worst of the scum we hunt shit their pants. Would make for an entertaining job working with you."

As much as I knew providing justice was necessary, that wasn't something I had ever thought to do as a full-time job. Something Dawsyn had commented on before and that I hadn't really thought too much about until she mentioned it was being a leader.

I didn't expect to be in charge, but I wanted to be

here, helping make the hard choices for our people. I knew there was going to be a long road ahead for Drago in order to get it back to the glory it once was, and I wanted to be part of that.

Though, I also knew I had to take into consideration what Dawsyn wanted. She and her family were close. The connection she had to her pack was strong, and I didn't want to take that from her. I just hoped there would be a way to compromise, giving us both what we needed to be happy besides each other.

Dawsyn and River shifted into their wolf forms and raced below my dragon as I took to the skies. It was the first time I'd been away from the caves since returning from killing Knox.

I half-expected more destruction, but besides the new damage near the mountain, everything appeared just as shitty as it had been before. Possibly even better if that was possible. Without the plumes of smoke everywhere, the town didn't seem as annihilated as I'd remembered.

We got to the portal, and I was the last to shift back, but as soon as I was on two feet again, I reached for Dawsyn without conscious thought. The need to have her close was stronger than it had ever been.

She glanced up at me with bright eyes. "Do you need to re-up your cloaking spell?"

I nodded and held an arm out in front of me, pushing scales to the surface and then plucking one from my skin.

I'd yet to do this in front of Dawsyn, and I didn't miss River's rapt attention on me either.

The spell was almost like the bonding process due to needing a bit of blood and a scale, something I hadn't really considered before, but with my mate so close...

I almost couldn't control my desire to nick her palm and shove the scale into her skin, marking her as mine.

With a rumble, I shook the thoughts away. I wouldn't force a connection on her, even if I felt confident that she wanted what we'd had back as badly as I did.

Instead, I extended my nails into claws, nicked the tip of one finger, then covered the scale lightly in my own blood.

As soon as that was done, I pulled the top of my shirt down and pressed the light-green scale to my chest.

Heat built inside me as the magic transformed the scale from a physical object to energy that embedded into my skin, spreading throughout the rest of my body with light tingles.

When I looked up, Dawsyn and River were both staring at me with fascination, but it was the former's I cared about most.

She stepped closer to me and laid her hand lightly over my chest where I'd just placed the scale beneath my shirt.

"I can feel the warmth of the energy," she said softly.

"It only lasts a few minutes, but the magic itself can last for up to a week." There was so much more I wanted to say and do, but River standing only ten feet away had me keeping those other thoughts and wants to myself. Just barely.

He coughed and stepped further back. "Alright. Well, how about that portal?"

I couldn't stop the smirk from appearing on my face. I had no doubt that he was sensing the sexual tension between Dawsyn and me, but I wasn't going to apologize for wanting my mate so thoroughly.

The want was more of a need that I didn't know how much longer I was going to be able to control.

Chapter Seven

DAWSYN

I'd already known that something was different with Cillian from the moment he'd walked out of that cave and kissed me senselessly. Still, the longer we were around each other, the more I could feel the tides changing.

The tension between us felt as if it was at a new high. One that I wanted to lose myself in and never come back from.

We need to bond with him, my wolf said.

I knew she was right, but I had still been holding out hope that our fated mate bond would return on its own and that completing a chosen mate connection wouldn't be necessary.

Though, at this point, anything was better than the cavernous hole between us. It felt so vast inside my chest, even though he was right here next to me.

The memory of the tether I'd once had to him—the one I'd taken for granted—weighed heavily on me, but I wasn't going to give up. Any bond with Cillian was better than no bond. I just had to keep reminding myself of that and have a talk with him about how he was feeling about our fucked-up situation as well.

Cillian pointed toward the opaque portal and nodded toward River. "After you."

When my best friend didn't budge, I had a feeling I'd scarred him for life after shoving him through before.

"I want to go first," I said, pushing up onto my toes and kissing Cillian quickly before forcing myself to leave his side.

He didn't seem thrilled with my idea, but I didn't want to embarrass River. Poking fun at him was a favorite of mine, but going past the point of making him uncomfortable wasn't enjoyable.

My body stayed straight as I stepped through the energy. Shivers raced over my skin as my body was sucked forward, thrusting me into a nothingness for the briefest of moments, then depositing me into the alcove of the large mountain base in Montana.

Nothing had changed from just an hour ago, and I stepped out of the way in time for River to come through with a glare on his face. "That was ridiculously simple. Pushing me before wasn't necessary."

"I know." A grin grew on my face. "But it was fun."

Cillian came through next, and we both reached a hand for the other, intertwining our fingers before heading for his truck that was still parked around the corner.

My phone pinged with a new message as I reached

for it to see if Ava was around to teleport us instead of driving.

Mom: You have a new cousin: Dominic Ash. He's the definition of perfection.

She sent through a picture with Dominic cradled in Aunt Lucy's arms. The purest of smiles was on my aunt's face, and I was glad I'd asked my parents not to tell her what was going on with me. Aunt Lucy deserved this moment, even if she hadn't thought she wanted children.

She was an incredible woman in her own unique ways, and she'd be the same as a mother.

Me: Give them both a hug and kiss from me and pass along my love. I wish I was there.

I received a response before I could even find Ava's name in my phone to text for a pick-up.

Mom: You're doing okay?

Me: Yep. River and Cillian are with me. We're headed to Spell House. I need to know what solutions GiGi has found for that spell.

Mom: She should be back there soon. I'll let her know you'll be waiting. Love you and keep us updated. We'll be there just as soon as you need us.

Me: Love you and will do.

"I forgot that GiGi wasn't at the coven at the moment," I said after I got done texting. "We'll have some time to kill once we get there."

River raised a finger. "We can go see Brixley."

Or he could go see Brixley, and I could have some time alone with my mate...

"Yes, you absolutely should do that," I said while sending Ava a message.

River groaned and walked further away from us. Cillian leaned against the side of his truck and reached for my hips as I slipped my phone back into my pocket.

"You don't want to go see your friend?" he asked me, fingers stroking against the skin just beneath the hem of my shirt.

"I will," I replied breathily. "Eventually. But I thought maybe we should talk some more."

I heard River's scoff. "Talk. Right. I can smell you from here."

"Then go further away," Cillian snarled before softening his gaze back at me. "I'm not opposed to *talking*."

I really hoped we were on the same fucking page for once. I'd tried getting him to go further several times before, yet there had always been a reason not to.

With GiGi away and River hopefully soon to be distracted...we might finally get what we'd both needed for weeks now. Bond be damned.

Cillian leaned his forehead against mine and lowered his voice until it was more of a grumble than anything else. "That witch better hurry or River won't be able to get far enough away fast enough."

The smirk that appeared on my face matched the joy that radiated through my heart.

We were absolutely on the same page. Halle-fucking-lujah.

Just as I pushed up to kiss him, I sensed Ava's magic filter through the air and let my shoulders sag.

Soon, we'd be alone. Very fucking soon.

I turned around and waved at Ava while staying within the hold Cillian had on me. "Thanks for coming."

Her shoulders shivered. "You're not welcome. Where's the boy?"

River appeared behind her. "The *man* is right here."

Even I had to laugh a little at that. Poor River needed to get out more so people could see the man he'd grown into. Until then, most of them just remembered the kid his parents used to bring around during gatherings.

Ava held both of her hands out. With Cillian still touching me, I reached for one and River took the other. Before I could tell her that I wanted to go to Spell House, the world went black and we reappeared at the coven-turned-community.

Even though it had been years since GiGi opened her home to other supernaturals and became the first official community in our hidden world, my parents had still so often called this place the coven that considering it as anything else was hard to remember.

"Beatrix wants you to wait here for her," Ava said. "She doesn't need anyone poking around her shit. Her words, not mine."

Of course, she didn't.

"Do you know if Brixley is here or at the pack?" River asked.

"I haven't seen her, so I'd check the pack," Ava answered, then turned to Cillian and me again. "You can wait in one of the guest cabins or walk around. I'm sure Beatrix will find you herself as soon as she returns, but it might be a few hours."

There was a lot we could do in a few hours.

"I have my phone," River said. "Call me when GiGi is back. If you leave without me, you're dead."

Cillian's chest rumbled, but I patted his arm. "He means that with all the love in the world, don't you, Riv?"

He shook his head at us. "Whatever you need to believe."

River took off in the opposite direction, and Ava disappeared to wherever else she needed to be.

I glanced up at my mate with hope in my eyes. "Would you like a tour of Earth's first supernatural community?"

"Not even in the slightest." The deep tenor of his words sent desire straight through me, and I didn't hesitate in grabbing his hand.

"Right this way, then." I led us down the cobblestone path between the guest cabins.

Over the years, half of them had been turned into homes for supernaturals to live in until they needed something bigger. More houses had also been built closer toward the forest area, but the cabins in this area had been around for as long as I could remember. GiGi had finally reinforced them with soundproof spells once more supernaturals began staying in her coven.

We approached the last row of cabins, and I went to the door of the middle one that had a vacant sign hanging from the bronze doorknob. I removed the sign and twisted the handle, peeking behind me.

Cillian was right there. His warmth penetrated my skin, and his eyes bored right into my soul. I licked my lips and felt my canines already extending. My chest rapidly rose and fell, sending shivers throughout my insides that gathered at my pulsing core.

I stood there wordlessly and in awe of how much I wanted this man. Wanted his heart, body, and soul. Needed all of him to be *mine*.

Fuck me. I needed him more than I could even comprehend.

His hands wrapped around my waist, lifting my feet from the ground. "Inside, Dawsyn. Now."

I kicked the door the rest of the way open behind me, and he carried me through the entryway before using his hip to slam the door closed.

"Lock it," I reminded him.

The last thing we needed was for my GiGi to walk in while we were naked. I couldn't imagine even my twisted grandmother finding humor in that situation.

He held me against his chest with one arm around my waist as his other hand reached for the lock, clicking it into place.

Inside, there was only a small kitchenette area on our right and a king-sized bed to our left with a small table set in the middle. Though, the only thing I could really focus on was the bed and how suddenly restrictive my clothes were feeling on my burning body.

"I don't want to assume that I know how you're

feeling," Cillian said gruffly. "We don't have to do anything here that you don't want to."

I pressed my hands to his chest, feeling his heart pounding beneath my touch. "Cillian, I was willing to fuck you in freezing water. Having you alone in a cabin that is magically soundproofed is like a dream come true. Now, get naked."

The left side of his mouth lifted, and his eyes sparked with emotions that went straight to my heart even before he spoke.

"I'm not going to fuck you, Dawsyn," he practically whispered, but the words felt so loud in my ears. "I'm going to love you with everything I have."

We hadn't said "I love you," and I wasn't sure I was ready for that kind of verbal declaration myself, but that didn't mean I didn't know in my heart that I had all the love for this man and would gladly accept whatever love he wanted to give me in return.

He was it for me. Mine for the rest of my days, no matter what had happened before or might happen in the future.

"Then, get naked *please*," I said as I lifted my shirt above my head, breathing heavily.

His responding growl went straight to my core, and I couldn't get our clothes off fast enough.

My wolf was right there with me, needy for our mate, but quiet. Given there were no talks about completing a bond yet, this was more about me and Cillian and our bodies than it was our spirits. Though, that didn't make the actions we were about to partake in any less powerful.

Cillian was glorious in his bare form. My eyes slowly slid from his face over his broad shoulders, down each of his muscled arms, then back up to his chest before going down again toward his stomach muscles which visibly rippled under my scrutiny.

My tongue darted out, wanting to trace the lines of his abs with the tip, but before I could drop to my knees, Cillian was picking me up and carrying me toward the bed.

I wrapped my legs around his waist and ground my naked body over his, eliciting a delicious groan from the back of his throat.

"I don't know how we waited so long," he complained.

I almost opened my mouth and pointed out the various reasons, but my mind was quicker than my tongue and kept those thoughts to myself.

He laid me on the bed, and I released him only long enough for him to crawl on top of me, aligning our hips before resting his elbows on each side of my shoulders so that his hands could still reach my face.

His thumbs stroked my neck, moving up my jawline as his lips peppered kisses around my eyes, then my cheeks, before landing on my mouth.

Our tongues met in the middle, tangling with sweet need, tasting each other until I couldn't tell where I ended and he began.

I reached between us, and his waist lifted, giving me access to the part of him I'd yet to be as acquainted with as I wanted to be.

My fingers wrapped around the silky skin of his hard cock, sliding up and down in perfect succession with his kisses.

He moved further up, breaking the kiss. "I can't wait any longer."

"Then don't."

We didn't need foreplay. We just needed each other. There was no reason to waste time with pomp and circumstance this first time.

That was what the rest of our lives were for, because it didn't matter that there was still a hole where his essence used to reside in me. I was never letting this man go again.

Using the hold that I already had on him, I guided the head of his dick toward my wet and waiting pussy, rubbing the tip against me before he thrusted forward.

Only a couple inches in and my chest expanded while my lungs sucked in a sharp breath of need.

He froze and searched my face. "Are you okay?"

I dug my nails into his asscheeks. "As long as you keep going, I am."

That had his smile returning and his hips resuming their previous movements. He rocked against me, and I lifted my legs until my hips rotated back, giving him room to go deeper.

Moments passed, but once he was fully seated inside me, all I could sense was Cillian—the thrum of his heartbeat, his every inhale and exhale, the heat of his skin, the feel of him not only above me, but inside me.

Nothing in my life had consumed me so thoroughly.

My mind could only focus on him. The emotions only he could elicit from me, the fresh earthy scent that was so uniquely his, the way my heart wanted to explode with joy.

He moved over me, playing my body as if he'd known me his whole life and I could only sing for him.

Our eyes locked, and I lifted my head to kiss him again, but just as our lips brushed against each other, electricity shot through my chest, burning my skin and not in a sexy way.

My mouth popped open, and my fingers rubbed over the spot that ached just as Cillian's eyes squeezed closed and he stopped moving above me.

I was about to ask him what the hell that was, but the scorching sensation stopped and in its place was...

Holy shit.

Holy fucking shit.

Our tether.

I couldn't stop the tears that leaked out the sides of my eyes from the joy it brought me.

My hands grasped on to Cillian's face, waiting briefly for his eyes to reopen. "Do you feel it?"

He nodded, his own eyes glossing over. "Our bond came back."

The roughness of his voice nearly shattered my heart in the best way possible. I kissed him again, the need between us only growing more rapidly. His increased thrusts showed me I wasn't the only one feeling the ecstasy of it all.

My skin pebbled all over my body, and my nails

clawed over his back as my orgasm hung just on the precipice of release. Only, I wasn't ready to lose myself to the euphoria. Not yet.

It didn't matter that Cillian wasn't a wolf. The need to mark him—to bond to him in the way that wolves bonded to each other—was too strong to ignore now that the tether was back and I could sense just how much he had truly come to care for me.

My canines elongated, and this time I didn't try to hide them. I peppered kisses along his jaw, letting the sharp points scrape over his skin until I got to his neck. I kissed him once, then ran my tongue over his salty skin right before I bit down, breaking the skin.

He didn't even flinch from the contact like I'd expected him to. Instead, his energy filtered through to me, not only from the tether between us, but also his blood while he rocked harder against me. His moans turned to growls, and his efforts weren't wasted.

I pulled back from his neck and let go of everything I'd been afraid of before, crying out his name and finding my release.

All I'd needed was Cillian, and now that I truly had him, I never again had to fear losing him.

Chapter Eight

CILLIAN

The outlines of scales littered my arms as the bond —the one I didn't believe I'd ever feel in the same way again—ignited in my chest. Dawsyn was there. Her essence, the rapid beat of her racing heart, the taste of her emotions. All of it was there, pulsing from her into me through the tether that only a few weeks ago had been turned to ash.

I wasn't sure if it was the sex, or our acceptance of the chosen mate bond, or something entirely different that brought our connection back.

However it happened, the power and strength that filled my chest and spread through the rest of my body as I rested over her, momentarily spent from the sex and the reappearance of our bond, had my mind spinning.

I wiped a stray tear from her cheek. "You feel it, too."

She nodded and grinned. "More than even before. Maybe because I marked you."

The mention of her biting me had my dick

hardening all over again. I hadn't expected her to do it and probably wouldn't have been excited about the idea if we'd talked about it beforehand. Yet, the moment her teeth scraped across my skin, I'd been done for.

Once she punctured my skin, it had taken everything in me not to find my release before she did.

I reached for her hand and rubbed my thumb over the center of her palm. "It's my turn to mark you."

There wouldn't be a physical mark from my scale, but even though we were fated mates and Dawsyn had accepted me in her wolf ways, I still needed to inject my magic inside her with a scale.

She frowned and pulled her hand back. "Not that one. This one."

I nearly asked her why, but then realized Knox had done this to her before. I wasn't the first dragon to claim her.

But, I'd be the only one to touch her for the rest of our lives, and that was what I chose to focus on. I couldn't lose myself to the rage again.

I tugged another scale from my forearm and gently grabbed her left hand, turning it over as I raised up more onto my knees, so I wouldn't squish her beneath my weight.

She watched me with enthralled attention. Her eyes were wide but intrigued as I rubbed my clawed nail over her skin. "Mind if I...do the honors?"

Her teeth scraped over her lower lip, and she nodded. "I wouldn't have it any other way."

I took the tip of my dragon claw and cut into her soft

palm with ease. Blood pooled in the center as I slid the scale over her hand and into the crimson liquid before pushing it deeper.

As soon as the two connected, her blood darkened, pulling the scale further into her body, then glowed the same light silver I'd seen her wolf do.

Dawsyn's eyes pinched closed, and her head tilted back on the mattress. "Mother shittery shit."

She didn't sound in pain. In fact, her voice was strangled with need, and her hips wiggled beneath me as her chest expanded.

"More than you expected?" I asked.

"So much fucking more."

I rubbed my thumb over the center of her palm that was already healing without a speck of blood to be seen. The moment I touched where the scale had disappeared, Dawsyn's eyes flew back open.

She reached for me and jerked my face down to hers, kissing me with a frenzied need that was even more powerful than before.

"I need you," she murmured against my lips.

Considering I was still seated inside her and already hard again, I had no problem complying with her request, but she had other plans.

Her hands pressed against my chest, forcing me to the side. I took her lead, moving until I was on my back and she was positioning herself over me.

She sank slowly over my cock, her mouth slightly open and head dropped back as she sighed with what I assumed to be relief.

"Fuck," she hissed. "Nothing, and I mean this literally, has ever felt this good."

My hands reached for her hips, and I rocked her forward. The gasp that left her lips let me know this wasn't going to take long, and I was going to take advantage of every moment.

I surged up inside her as she began to ride me with abandon.

She leaned forward, pressing her hands over my chest to use as leverage. Once her hips were moving at their own rhythm, I trailed my fingers up her sides until they could cup her full breasts.

I pinched both nipples until they hardened, and she tensed above me, biting her lip again.

Her pussy tightened around the base of my cock, and I had to grit my teeth. She was right. Nothing had ever been like this—being with her, holding her in my arms, claiming her and knowing that she was mine. Now and always.

The tether between us grew and solidified as the magic from my scale moved through her body. There wasn't a physical sign that our bond was now complete, but as she moved over me, holding on to me, shattering all her internal walls, I knew without a doubt in my mind that it was done.

Dawsyn was everywhere inside me now. Her heart beat in time with mine, and her emotions mingled inside me, enhancing the need I had for her.

My chest expanded until I thought it might explode, then she looked right into my eyes and everything settled.

Every racing thought and emotion clicked into its place, and I knew nothing would ever be more perfect than she was for me.

Within minutes, she was collapsing into my arms, and my body shuddered beneath hers, holding on tightly and never wanting this moment to end.

Her head rested against my chest, our breathing continuing to match pace. "I could stay here forever."

Hell, even our thoughts seemed to match.

"We'll stay here for as long as you want," I said.

"Forever wouldn't be long enough."

I knew exactly what she meant.

She started to get up, but I pressed my hands over her spine, holding her to me. "Not yet."

"People are counting on us," she reminded me.

"Fuck the people."

Her laugh vibrated through my body. "I love that you want to be selfish with me again. Even more than that, I'm so fucking thankful our bond wasn't lost for good, but we really should be ready when my GiGi gets back. We only have three days, Cillian."

I heard everything she was saying. I understood all of it, but that didn't mean I was ready to break away from this moment.

We were bonded. The connection no longer lingered between us, it flared to life, ebbing and flowing between our souls, tying us together for a lifetime.

This wasn't something I was going to rush. Not even for the world.

I held her tighter in my arms until her body relaxed. "Five more minutes."

"Or hours," I mused.

She tried shaking her head, but I kept her firmly against me.

We laid there together—her on top of me, me still inside her. Us, together as one. The longer we stayed skin-to-skin as we were, the stronger I felt our bond grow.

The tether no longer felt like it went straight from her heart to mine. Instead, the cord moved throughout our bodies, marking each of our souls with a brand from the other.

I had no clue how much time had passed, but by the time I was willing to release Dawsyn, she was breathing evenly over my body and her face was slack.

My hands gently rubbed over her back, and she groaned. "Not sleeping, just not alive."

I smirked, knowing exactly how she felt.

"We can stay as long as you want," I repeated my earlier sentiments, but they had the opposite effect on my mate.

She leaned up, and this time I didn't stop her. "We should get up."

"If you say so." I watched her crawl off me and stand gloriously naked beside the bed without a care in the world.

Her hands fell to her hips as she glanced at the floor. "What did you do with my underwear?"

"I'm pretty sure you were the one ripping clothes off," I replied with a wink. "They're here somewhere."

I got up and helped her look for everything we'd stripped off earlier. It wasn't until I went to the kitchen area that I found her underwear. In the sink.

"Got them." I plucked them from the basin and held them between my fingers, higher than she could reach without jumping.

She raised a brow. "Don't tempt me to go commando. I'll do it."

I knew she would, then all I'd be thinking about was her bare pussy beneath her jeans...

Without waiting long, I dropped the cotton fabric into her outstretched hand, then smacked her ass. "Get dressed."

I'd already done so as we were looking for her clothes but still needed to put my boots back on. I sat at the small table and was only halfway done lacing them up when Dawsyn stood in front of me and pushed her index finger into my forehead, forcing me to sit up straighter.

When there was room for her, she straddled my lap, dressed only in her shirt and underwear. Her hands cupped my face, and she pressed two quick kisses to my lips. "I heart you."

They weren't the words I would have used, but in a way, they were very Dawsyn.

I knew my mate felt big emotions, but she wasn't a fan of them. It was the only reason I'd yet to tell her how I truly felt. Though, I also knew that she didn't need words from me. She knew what she needed to know by my actions.

"I heart you, too," I replied easily with a grin on my face.

"Good," she said. "I might have stabbed you otherwise."

She was standing back up in the next second, and I was pulsing with joy as I resumed tying up my boots.

This woman was going to keep me on my toes for the rest of my life, and I couldn't be happier about it.

Within a few minutes, we were both dressed, and Dawsyn used her fingers to comb her hair into submission. Once she deemed herself presentable, she glanced at the door, then back at me. "When we walk out of this cabin, I don't know when we'll get another moment alone."

I closed the distance between us in two strides and held her shoulders. "If we choose to believe Estelle, we'll have all the time we need in just a few days. Either because we're dead or because Knox is."

She shoved me. "Don't put shit like that into the universe. There is only one goal here: to stop Knox. Nothing else is possible, do you hear me?"

I did, loud and clear. "You're right. We haven't come this far to lose."

"Fuck no, we haven't." She huffed then turned for the door, but I grabbed her wrist before she could twist the handle.

I tugged her back to my chest and kissed her once

more, my tongue sliding between her lips, opening her mouth to me and tasting her sweetness that was all mine.

Her essence was mingled with my dragon magic, and that had my need to protect her growing exponentially.

"Maybe we should stay here a while longer," I murmured.

She shoved me back. "Not a chance in hell, lover boy."

I had to grin, or I was going to rage. There was no in between. And grin I did, because I knew as I watched her walk out of the cabin that I would never hesitate with Dawsyn again.

I would kill every single threat that came our way. That included my brother.

Chapter Nine

DAWSYN

Having the alpha gene didn't always mean I made the right choices or did the things an alpha would, mostly because I was certain I still had many years to prepare for the day when I'd need to come home and take over my pack.

Though, there were times—like now—when lives were on the line and as much as I wanted to be selfish by staying with Cillian, I knew we couldn't. I knew that I wouldn't be able to live with myself if people died because we'd chosen ourselves over trying to protect not only the lives of the dragons, but their world.

Hell, at that point, it seemed as if it wasn't just Drago's future we needed to be worried about. If we failed to stop Knox from coming into his true power, from rising out of the ashes stronger than ever before, then Earth would be his next target.

I doubted he intended to destroy this place unless he also had a true death wish, but I bet he wanted to wreak

"

enough havoc that all would bow to him. I wouldn't let that happen. Not while I was capable of stopping him.

Cillian caught up to me when I was only a few feet from the cabin. His fingers entwined with mine as we walked together toward GiGi's home, but before we could get there, she appeared in front of us.

"Good, you figured your shit out," she said, then grinned. "I can't wait to see Roman's face when he knows."

I rolled my eyes. "It's not like he doesn't know I've had sex before. I've been in heat."

GiGi's eyes sparked with mischief. "Oh, there are ways to survive a heat without sex. I'm sure your father's convinced himself you did just that." She pointed to the two of us and scrunched her nose up, likely smelling the change in our scents. "But now, there's no denying you're bonded."

Cillian's body twisted, almost as if he was trying to block me from my grandmother. "What about the spell? Did you find a solution to the last ingredient?"

She snapped her fingers, and a stream of silver energy zapped him in the chest. "Don't you know not to talk about certain things in public, boy?" She tsked. "I still can't decide if I like you."

The last bit was said more as if she was speaking to herself, so neither of us bothered to reply.

"Should we head to Spell House?" I asked.

She nodded, then glanced around. "Evelyn is waiting for us. She took over for me while I was needed in Fae Islands."

Evelyn wasn't the friendliest of witches, but she was the second most powerful witch in this community. At least, last I'd heard. Hopefully she'd found something in the last couple of days.

GiGi opened a portal, this time to the attic at Spell House. When we stepped through, there were more tables out and books everywhere, along with bottles, boxes, and bags filled with things I tried not to look too closely at.

Some of the crazy shit they used in spells were better left unknown.

Cillian's nose turned up, and I nudged him. "Try not to inhale or figure out what anything is. You'll thank me later."

"Noted," he replied gruffly.

GiGi headed around the table to where Evelyn was working. "Do you have the notes for them?"

The elder witch nodded, tugging briefly at her white hair that was braided to the side. Then, she patted a paper next to her without really looking up. "It's all right here."

"I thought you only needed one more item?" Cillian asked.

Both witches snapped their heads up, Evelyn's hazel eyes glaring hardest at my mate. Though, it was GiGi who spoke. "Do not ever question our methods when you need our help."

Power pulsed through the room, and visible energy sparked around both elder witches.

Cillian swallowed thickly. "Understood."

GiGi picked up the paper and handed it to me.

"Because the Ginlic referenced in the book you had isn't grown anymore and we don't have time to conjure seeds and hope they're correct, we'll need to substitute the plant for a couple other things, but they need to be sourced. Considering I've been gone from the community way too much lately, the two of you are going to need to go hunting."

Two of us… Shit.

"We forgot about River," I said. "He went to see Brixley, but he'll be coming with us."

GiGi ignored my statement, likely uncaring since it didn't change what needed to be done. "I need a mushroom grown deep in the south of Louisiana swamps. It's dangerous to get, not only because of the supernaturals that frequent there, but because the swamp is…disgusting, but I'm sure you'll be fine. You might smell funny when you come back, but that will go away in time."

I tried to hold back my grimace. "What about the other item?"

"If you can succeed with the mushroom task, then the other will be pie," GiGi replied, making me shake my head at her use of "pie" instead of "cake."

She continued, "This only tells of the mushroom. I'll give you more direction if you can manage this measly task."

I glanced at the paper, and there was a hand-drawn picture of the fungi, blue in color with pale green speckles on top. It was taller than it was wide with a skinny stem that GiGi pointed to.

"You cannot break that stem. Dig the roots out and bring it back whole or else it won't work."

Cillian pointed to a glass jar. "Mind if I take that to put it in?"

"Now you're being smart." She grabbed the jar in question, holding it between her palms, then muttered a few words I didn't understand. A silver glow encased the glass, then she handed it to my mate. "It will take more force than you should encounter to break this, but it can still be lost or stolen. Don't be that dumb, okay?"

"I'll do my best," he deadpanned.

She patted his hand as he grabbed the jar. "I'm sure you will."

One look at Cillian and I could tell he wanted to bite her head off, but she was my GiGi. She could be as obnoxious as she wanted, and he wouldn't touch her. As long as she wasn't putting me in danger.

"So, we can go now?" I asked. "I'd like to hopefully finish this early and bring back things for the dragons. The last supply run was interrupted, and they're running short on a lot of stuff."

"Such an alpha," GiGi said, already turning away from me, though it didn't sound like a compliment. "But please go. There's still plenty of work to be done by the rest of us while you're frolicking in the swamp."

She said that as if we were going on vacation. Maybe to her it would feel like one, but I'd been to a swamp before. I knew better. This was going to be worse than when I'd first arrived in Drago and thought my skin was going to melt off before I could adjust to the different climate.

"Am I still permitted to call on Ava?" I was already turning toward the stairs to leave the traditional way, but my grandmother sighed and walked over to us before I could lift the door to get back downstairs.

"I'll open a portal to the pack," she said. "Get River, say hello to Brixley and remind her she owes me a chat, then call Ava. She'll be ready to take you via portal so that none of you get stuck somewhere you shouldn't be, but don't make her wait long. That's rude."

Of course I knew that last bit, but I was a little surprised GiGi did as well.

She pressed her hands together, creating the energy needed to get us to the wolf pack that had remained close yet still separate from the community residing in the witch coven.

With quick movements, the portal opened in front of the oversized wooden house, and we stepped through before GiGi could chastise us for being slow.

As soon as it closed behind us, a rumble echoed from Cillian's chest. "She's very lucky you love her so dearly."

"I see you've become acquainted with Beatrix," a familiar voice said from behind us. "I nearly choked the life out of her during some of our first meetings so I can understand your sentiments."

I turned around to see Uncle Foster standing there, arms loose at his sides, tattoos on display like usual, and dressed casually in jeans and a t-shirt. He brushed his shoulder-length hair back, then opened his arms. "It's been a while, kid."

I nodded and accepted the welcome gesture, hugging him tightly in return. "It has."

"And I see a lot has changed." There was a bit of tension in his voice. "Roman mentioned that you'd found your mate, but he didn't..."

"He doesn't know," I said when I pulled back. "And he doesn't need to. He and Mom are with Finn and Lucy."

Uncle Foster stepped forward and shook Cillian's hand. "Welcome to our pack. I assume you're Cillian." Then, he sniffed the air. "Interesting how you can do that with your scent."

"It isn't without practice," Cillian answered.

"I hope you're well practiced in more than concealing yourself." Uncle Foster nodded at me. "You have some rather cared-for cargo in your possession and several packs who will hunt you down if anything happens to her."

Both a groan and a growl came from my throat. "Well, it was lovely seeing you, but we really need to be going."

His responding chuckle only served to make me realize I'd reacted just how he'd hoped. "River and B are at the treehouse. I'll let her know you're headed that way."

The treehouse? Hell, I hadn't been there since... I couldn't even remember when.

"You have houses in trees?" Cillian asked as we

walked away from my uncle.

I tried to hide my grin, so that he didn't get embarrassed thanks to Drago and Earth being just different enough.

"It's more like a child's playhouse that was built into the tree," I said. "You'll see. It's not far past the pack house, which is that monstrosity there."

The massive log house sat at the end of a main gravel road. It was two stories tall with tree trunks holding up a second-story porch and a massive A-frame-style main window at the center of the home. Wooden chairs were placed along the porches, and I recalled sitting in them as a kid, dangling my feet, hating how I couldn't touch the ground for the longest time.

"Not that I'm upset or surprised," Cillian started, "but should I be concerned with the amount of people your parents told about me?"

I was shaking my head before he even finished asking. "They would have only told their closest friends, which are more family than friend. None of them will say anything to anyone that doesn't absolutely need to know. Hell, even my parents probably only said something so that the others would be at the ready if we needed them."

He took the information well and didn't press further on the subject, which gave me a relief I didn't expect.

The thought of choosing between my family and mate wasn't a pleasant one. Though, I had no doubts—especially after recent events—what that choice would be, even if it would break my heart.

"How many people live there?" Cillian asked as we walked past the large home.

"I have no clue, but there are thousands of wolf shifters in this area," I said. "Los Angeles, where we are now, is one of the biggest cities in the United States, humans and supernaturals included."

"Drago doesn't have cities, but we have territories," he replied. "Where we were is the only civilized area. Other dragons live elsewhere, but we have no way to communicate with them unless we send a messenger, which I'm pretty sure we haven't been able to spare given all the chaos. They'll have no clue they're about to die should Knox wake before we think."

That wasn't going to happen, but the thought did have my stride increasing.

Within five minutes, we'd made it to the treehouse. When I couldn't see River or Brixley, I knew they were up the twenty-foot-tall ladder.

"I hope you're not afraid of heights," I teased Cillian, but he didn't find me as funny as I did.

"I'm a flying dragon," he deadpanned. "I think I can handle climbing a tree, and shouldn't I be the one saying that to you?"

His brow raised, but I wasn't bothered. "Flying with very little to hold on to is different from going up a ladder."

A rumble echoed from his chest. "Very little, huh?"

I shrugged and winked, merely because annoying him still brought me joy even if I cared about him a hell of a lot more than I did when I first met him. "I said what I said."

"I think I proved I have more than a little of everything earlier," he replied with a sexy growl.

That he did, but this was a conversation to be continued later.

I started up the ladder and grinned when I looked up to see Brixley's smiling face.

Her blonde hair fell in soft curls around her shoulders, and her light-brown eyes stood out starkly beneath her long lashes.

"It's about time you showed up," she said. "River was boring me about his classes and trying to convince me to join him at the academy."

"Actually," I said as I pulled myself onto the landing, "that's not the craziest idea he's ever had."

Her shoulders dropped. "Seriously? Not you, too."

I moved to make sure that Cillian had enough room to join us, then quickly remembered we were no longer children. Having four adults up here was not the same as a group of kids growing up.

We managed to squeeze in together, me ending up in Cillian's lap while Brixley and River sat across from us. "Seriously," I said to her. "You may not have wanted to talk about it, but I can tell you're struggling here. The people at the academy are actually pretty nice. Nobody there would give a shit that you're a hybrid. Hell, the women threw themselves at Cillian and thought he was one."

"I'm still mad Brixley knew that wasn't true before

me," River cut in, but I ignored him. He wasn't allowed to be upset by that anymore.

"Regardless, give it some thought," I told her. "Especially if you're still coming up here to hide."

She narrowed her eyes. "I'm not hiding. It's where I can think best."

"Because you're not around people," I added.

"How about your mate bond?" she asked, changing the subject on me. "I'm glad I was wrong about the chosen mate thing."

I grimaced. Apparently, nobody had filled Brixley in. Though, anyone that could have wouldn't have known the role she'd played in all this earlier on.

"Actually, you weren't," I said, then as briefly and quickly as I could explained the whole Knox situation. At least, the parts she needed to know about. "We actually need to get going." I glanced at River. "We need to get to Louisiana."

"The swamp, more specifically," Cillian said. "A place Beatrix made sound...interesting."

River grimaced. "That doesn't sound like it's going to be a pleasant experience."

"I haven't seen anything else about your situation," Brixley said. "I'm not sure if that's a good thing or not."

I let out a sigh. "Let's pretend it's the best thing ever."

Thinking anything else wasn't an option I wanted to consider. All I was going to focus on for the time being was finding the mushroom, then figuring out wherever else we had to go in the short time we had.

Chapter Ten

CILLIAN

Dawsyn stayed in the treehouse with Brixley for a bit longer while I headed back down with River. When we were standing there waiting, he appraised me heavily.

"I didn't think you were good enough for Dawsyn when I first found out you were mates," he said pointedly. "I hated that you were different, because I knew it would cause her problems she shouldn't have to deal with."

Apparently, he wasn't pulling punches today.

"Then, when she was taken, I wanted to kill you," he continued. "I only didn't because I knew Dawsyn would never forgive me. Still, I hoped when she was found that she'd leave you and we'd find a way to reject your bond."

"Are you trying to make me want to return the sentiments?" I said with a snarl, my fingers twitching at my sides and wanting to wrap around his throat.

River was my mate's best friend, but I wasn't going

to tolerate him joining us if he didn't support what we were fighting for.

He shook his head and smiled. "I just want all the cards on the table. Dawsyn loves you, which means you're family to me now. Seeing her earlier for the first time since she was taken, I could understand that it didn't matter how much I hated that she'd been put into danger. I was going to do whatever it took to support the two of you, because that's what she needs."

"So, you dislike me, but are willing to put those feelings aside to support your best friend?" I asked through gritted teeth, trying to be quiet to prevent Dawsyn from getting upset.

A line deepened between his brows. "No, not at all. Shit, I didn't say any of that right."

"What the fuck are you trying to say then, River?"

"I'm glad she has you even though I hated you at first," he replied quickly. "I can sense how much she means to you, and none of what happened before matters. I'm here to make sure that you two get what you want and deserve. In a good way."

"You probably could have left the rest of that stuff out." I didn't need to know that he'd once wanted to kill me. Did he have a reason—one that I agreed with because I'd even hated myself for letting Dawsyn be taken by Knox? Sure, but River needed to learn to keep some thoughts to himself.

"Probably, but that's not how Dawsyn and I stay so close," he said. "I figured I should give you the same courtesy."

I wasn't going to call what he'd done a *courtesy*, but I could at least appreciate that he was trying to be my friend.

"Glad we could get all that out of the way then," I muttered.

"All of what out of the way?" Dawsyn asked as she jumped to the ground next to me.

I reached for her, pulling her body into my side and kissing the side of her head. "Agreeing that keeping you safe is the most important thing here."

She shoved me away and lifted her lip. "Don't for one fucking second think that the two of you are going to gang up on me, trying to 'protect' me. I will kick both of your asses."

That had me grinning. "No ganging up was mentioned, but now that you've given us the idea..." I glanced at River. "We could probably lock her up somewhere safe if we worked together."

He nodded and stroked his chin. "I know this place where—"

Dark golden energy wrapped around him, cutting off his words, then Brixley stepped between the three of us. "If you do one thing against Dawsyn's will, you'll soon find out all the things I've recently learned when it comes to magic. In case you think that's an empty threat, GiGi has been teaching me personally."

I couldn't see her face, but the way River's throat bobbed, I'd assume Brixley was showing a side of herself that her friends had never seen before.

Dawsyn reached for the young witch. "Easy, B. I

think he's got the point. Though, if you can do that to Riv, I'd love to see what you could do to the fuckers who have been talking shit."

I saw the drop of Brixley's shoulders as she released River then turned to Dawsyn. "That's different. I wouldn't have really hurt River."

"How the hell is that different?" Dawsyn demanded. "If you can defend yourself, then you should."

Brixley lost all confidence and lowered her eyes. "I don't want to hurt them and prove I'm the freak they say I am."

The rumble in my mate's chest made me proud. "If you did hurt them, it wouldn't be anything they didn't deserve. I swear to the Gods, Brixley. If you haven't rectified your situation by the time I'm done with mine, I will come back here and literally bite all their heads off."

That had the witch's lips twitching. "Thanks, D. I've missed you guys."

River threw his arms around both of them. "We won't let so much time go by again, especially now that you're an adult."

From that comment and the youthfulness of Brixley's face, I realized she must have been several years younger than them, and I was glad she wasn't coming with us. I didn't want to be responsible for any other lives.

They hugged and said their goodbyes quietly.

"Do you want me to take you to Louisiana?" Brixley asked, seeming hopeful to help.

Dawsyn glanced back at me with a grimace on her face that her friend couldn't see.

"Can you open a portal and close it quickly?" I asked. "Beatrix mentioned Ava would be using one to lessen the chances of getting stuck somewhere we don't want to be."

She nodded eagerly, brushing her long blonde hair back. "I've been doing that for months now. Where do you need to be exactly?"

Dawsyn pulled the paper Beatrix had given us out from her back pocket, then pointed to the top. "This is the name of the swamp area."

Brixley reached for her phone and started typing, then rotated her screen, seeming to zoom in on something. "I can get you right about here if that works?"

When she turned the phone around, I saw she was showing Dawsyn a map. "That should be great."

The young witch took a few steps back, closing her eyes, and pressed her hands together. A sheer layer of the same dark gold magic coated her skin before she thrusted her hands forward, moving her palm in a circular motion.

It seemed as if she was putting forth a lot more effort than I'd seen Beatrix and Ava use, but I assumed ease came with age.

The portal opening grew wide and tall enough for us to walk through in single file. River approached first and stuck his head in. "It smells like ass, but I don't scent anything supernatural."

That didn't mean much. I knew I wasn't the only one who could hide their true identity. Still, I followed Dawsyn through the portal and was glad to see it closed by the time I started scanning the area.

We were standing on land, but it was soft and sinking beneath my weight. Each step squished under my feet, and the further we walked, the more I felt a heaviness pressing in around me. "What the hell is in the air here besides the smell?"

Dawsyn coughed and pinched her nose. "The humidity. You thought Texas was horrid. This is where the devil lives."

"I hope not literally," River grumbled, hands out in front of him and walking carefully. "How the hell are we supposed to find this mushroom?"

He glanced back as he asked that question, then screeched loud enough to make sure anyone within a few miles knew exactly where we were.

"What the fuck is that?" he bellowed, swiping at the air.

"I maybe should have mentioned the spiders," Dawsyn said with a wicked grin. "They like to build webs between the trees to catch their prey. Not just little bugs, either. Birds and shit."

She seemed all too pleased with this knowledge.

"How do you know all this?" I asked, staying right where I was until we had a more solid plan.

She nodded to the left. "My territory isn't too far from here. Texas is the next state over and I've been near these areas enough to learn a few things the hard way."

"Apparently, I've only been to the five-star swamps before this," River muttered, clearly disappointed he'd been caught off guard.

Croaking noises started from who knew what and were just loud enough to annoy me. "What else did the paper say about this mushroom?"

Dawsyn handed me the information. "Just that we'll find it growing in the shadows. It's something that actually hates sunlight."

"Great," River groaned. "You know what else hates sunlight."

Vampires.

Though, they didn't scare me, and I had no qualms about shifting at this point if I had to. Keeping dragons a secret was the least of my worries. Though, I'd keep my shield up as long as possible to avoid attracting anyone to us that was curious about a new scent.

Dawsyn smacked herself several times on each of her arms. "I think we'll need to be more concerned with the mosquitoes than the vampires."

I held the paper up, showing River the mushroom. "This is what we're looking for."

A tall plant with faint green spots placed sporadically over the upper half and what looked to be a delicate stem.

"Got it," he replied. "Just to be clear, we're looking for a needle in a swamp, right? If this mushroom was easy to find, it would be sold somewhere that we could have just gone and bought it."

Dawsyn grimaced. "Assumingly so."

"We need to stick together," I said before anyone could suggest splitting up.

I had no intention of letting Dawsyn out of my sight, and sending River off on his own probably wouldn't sit well with her.

"I agree," River said. "Just keep your eyes moving and senses out for anyone else that doesn't belong. We have no idea who could be hiding out here."

I had a feeling after what we'd seen and smelled already, it wasn't the "who" we needed to be worried about, but the "what".

The ground continued to get softer the further we walked, and there was no walking in a straight line since the water was everywhere around us. All the trees seemed to be the same, but I had no clue what they were.

The trunks were smooth and without bark. Branches were mostly covered in what appeared to be dead foliage. The nearly grey material draped down everywhere and thick enough that there was no way to tell what might be hiding beneath its web.

River kept the lead, and Dawsyn remained between us as we walked in a straight line. My eyes moved between the shadows and the area around us. All I saw was green and brown mush.

Breathing was limited, not only because of the humidity, but because the further we walked into the trees, the worse the smell wafting from the water.

"I wonder how many dead bodies are in that water," Dawsyn mused as if she'd known I was already thinking about the atrocious water. Then, she squealed. "Oh, look! A baby turtle."

Before I could stop her, she bent down, not seeing that the baby wasn't alone.

Its mother was just a foot behind it with the mouth of a killer bird, ready to take my mate's arm off.

Chapter Eleven

DAWSYN

Just as I reached for the baby turtle, an arm wrapped around my waist and jerked me against a hard chest.

"What the fuck?" I snapped at Cillian when I glanced up at him.

"Exactly my thought." He pointed his other hand toward the ground. "Where there are babies, there are usually mothers, Dawsyn."

Mother shittery shit.

I'd somehow missed that there was a hundred-pound killer turtle just mere inches behind the baby. Her beaked mouth was open and ready to attack as Cillian inched us further back, then released me.

"No more petting animals, even if they look harmless," he growled while also stroking the back of his hands down my arms.

"It would have been a little funny after she healed," River said with a chuckle that cut off quickly before he added, "I mean, be fucking careful, D."

I glanced up at Cillian to find him glaring at my best friend. My fist met his stomach. "Don't be such a bully."

"Don't put yourself in unnecessary danger," he droned.

I wasn't going to admit it out loud, but he sort of had a point.

While I was worried about the other supernaturals we might find out here, there also wasn't a shortage of wildlife in the swamp that would love to eat us for dessert.

We continued, all the while holding our breath to avoid taking in as much of the stench as possible, but also wanting to plug our ears from unending sounds of the frogs and what I assumed to be crickets. That combined with the mosquitoes that seemed to only want my blood, I was eager for a vicious vampire or something to come along.

Anything to distract me from the hell this swamp felt like.

"Uh-oh," River said. "We have a problem."

"Thank fuck," I muttered, earning myself another glare from my mate.

"What is it?" Cillian asked.

River pointed just a few feet in front of him where I could easily see the problem. "We either need to head back out of the swamp or we're going in the water."

"Maybe there's a boat somewhere we can borrow," I said, looking but not seeing anything useful.

"Doubtful," Cillian replied. "We'll head back north

away from the water, moving East as much as we can as the water changes."

"GiGi's paper was very specific about only going North once we entered the forest," I pointed out.

"Well, GiGi isn't here, is she?" River said, eyes scanning the area. "I agree with Cillian. None of us need to be in that water. We wouldn't be able to see any mushrooms growing in that murky deathtrap anyway. We're better off following it around."

"Whatever you two say." Something wasn't sitting right with me, so I checked in with my wolf.

This is a lose-lose situation, she replied. *Just agree with them and hopefully this will be less of a loss than wading into snake-infested waters.*

I shivered at the mention of snakes. There were very few things in this world that I was afraid of. Slithering, tongue-hissing reptiles were one of them.

I thought that once we got the bond back with Cillian that you'd be around more, I said to her. *Is everything okay?*

I'm still considering the new power inside us, she answered. *It's lessened since bonding with Cillian, and I don't understand why.*

It wasn't something I'd realized given everything that had been going on, but now that she'd said as much, I couldn't help noticing.

There had been a charge of energy at my core where I accessed my shifter power. It had been there when I raced River in Drago, yet the steady thrum was more of a quiet hum inside me.

As much as I appreciated having the boost of power while fighting the dragons, this isn't the end of the world, I said. *I wouldn't stress over it. Let's just find this mushroom. How do you feel about shifting and trying to sniff it out?*

I'm willing to run through this swamp, but that means splitting up from Cillian, she pointed out. *He shouldn't be shifting out here. Plus, with all the bog stench, it's not likely I'd sense anything on my own before you would.*

She made good points, but ones that slightly disappointed me as we started moving East. Yes, I considered myself and my wolf one and often referred to us as the same person, especially when shifted, but getting my human feet out of the sludge of the swamp didn't sound so terrible.

Cillian's arm shot out in front of me, pausing my forward momentum. "Be still."

His words were barely a whisper that had the hair on the back of my neck standing. I didn't bother to ask what he sensed. Instead, I searched with my eyes, ears, and nose, trying to locate it for myself.

There was a rustle in the branches to the southwest of us, but also a heartbeat in the water.

We weren't alone. I sniffed again. Two wolf shifters.

For a moment, I'd thought maybe it was just going to be nature trying to kill us today and not supernaturals.

How fortunate.

Scales appeared on Cillian's outstretched arms, surprising me even more as I sensed his shield dropping.

Apparently, he'd lost his give-a-damn and didn't tell me.

A figure dropped from the trees, and I thought for sure he was going to take down River, but my best friend wasn't without his skills as he'd proven several times lately.

River dropped low, narrowly missing the fist that was aimed for his face, then kicked out a leg, forcing the attacker to the ground. Cillian was right there with River, grabbing the guy by the neck, lifting him out of the mud, and almost choking the life out of him.

Except that guy wasn't alone. I sensed someone behind me and shifted quickly into my wolf form.

The much-too-rapid transformation made my bones ache and skin feel like it was being shredded to the point of never coming back together, but when I caught sight of the other man standing behind me, muscles bulging from his black shirt and hands shifted to claws, I knew I'd made the right decision.

My jaws snapped, and the growl that echoed from me and through the swamp had everyone pausing their movements.

As excited as I was about the prospect of being something more like my mother, I knew deep down that I was still more than capable as just me.

The guy that had been behind me stepped closer, and Cillian snarled, his energy warming my back. "You'll be dead before your claws have the chance to come within two inches of her if you take another step."

"What are you?" the guy's grumbling voice asked.

"None of your fucking business," my mate replied.

The guy in front of me scoffed. "Given it's my job to patrol this swamp, I'd say it is."

I didn't remove my eyes from him, but I sensed River moving closer just before he walked past me, shining a light from his phone on the man we hadn't touched yet.

He was dressed in all black, and my gaze zeroed in on the insignia on his chest. Two stakes crossed over each other with a dagger pointing up the middle.

Fuck. These were protectors from one of Aunt Amersyn and Uncle Maciah's crews.

I immediately shifted back to my human form as River began patting the guy down, then I asked, "Who is your supervisor?"

That was a trick question. None of the protectors were supervisors. Everyone reported directly to Amersyn or Maciah, and to be sure this guy hadn't just stolen the uniform from a dead body, I was going to ask a few questions.

He looked me up and down, garnering a growl from Cillian. "Maciah. He's in charge—"

I cut him off. "Why are you posted out here?"

"He wanted us to make sure the nest of vampires that we disbanded a few weeks ago here hadn't regathered after we left," the guy answered, his arms being jerked behind his back courtesy of River.

I glanced at my best friend. "Anything?"

"Nothing that isn't standard issue," River replied.

He would know what the protectors were supposed to have on their person from his schooling, so I trusted his assessment.

I turned to Cillian. "Let him go."

"What?" my mate growled. "Why?"

"Because they work for my aunt and uncle." As soon as the words left my mouth, I saw the eyes of the one Cillian was holding widen and his body further tense.

Cillian did as I asked, but not gently. The other guy landed face first in the mud.

As much as I was glad to see my mate not drowning in grief, I'd almost forgotten how abrasive he could be. Though, I didn't mind Rough Cillian...

"Are you Roman's daughter?" the shifter not wiping stank mud from his face asked.

I nodded and reached for Cillian. "I'm Dawsyn. This is my mate Cillian, and that's River Pierce. He'll be joining your ranks soon."

"I'm Kyler," he said, then nodded at the other guy. "That's Zach. What are you doing out here?"

His tone was only a little less hostile than before.

"Looking for something," Cillian answered, clearly still untrusting of these people.

"We're here to find a plant for Beatrix," I said. It didn't matter that we didn't know these shifters personally. They would have been fully vetted before becoming protectors working on their own. I trusted my aunt and uncle's process, which meant we could trust the men just enough to possibly have some help and maybe not sleep in the swamp tonight.

Kyler tensed briefly, then nodded. "Beatrix sent you? How can we help?"

"By staying out of our way," Cillian said, and I chuckled, pressing a hand over his arm.

Our stares met, and I silently pleaded with him to calm the fuck down. I might have been to the swamp before, but help wasn't a bad thing with all the creatures swarming around us, and I didn't just mean supernatural ones.

His lips thinned and he shook his head minutely.

"Cillian." I spoke his name softly but with an edge, and his responding sigh was exactly what I expected.

"Fine, but if either one of them even looks at you wrong, I will tear both their heads off." As he spoke the threat, he made sure to glance at both protectors. Though, only Zach's eyes cast downward. Kyler didn't seem as frightened, telling me that he'd likely seen some shit in his day. Death wasn't something he was afraid of.

"My mate isn't from around here," I explained, not just because of Cillian's attitude and protectiveness, but because he'd also partially shifted. Which meant he'd let his dragon energy run free. Something I was sure none of us had missed.

"Noted," Kyler said.

River moved behind me and took the drawing of the mushroom from my pocket. "We need to find this."

Without touching the paper, both Kyler and Zach inspected it for several seconds then glanced at each other.

"We've never seen that before," Zach said.

"Let's hope that's because you weren't looking for it

and not because it no longer exists," I said. Though, they both kept their focus on River instead of me or Cillian.

"Let's split up since there are more of us," Cillian said, and I had no doubt that was for selfish reasons more than anything else.

River didn't seem to be opposed to the suggestion, so I kept my thoughts to myself. For the moment.

"I have my phone," my best friend said. "Call if you find anything and I'll do the same."

I reached out and gave him a hug. It was something I didn't always do when we parted ways, but with the way things had been going and where we were...my heart needed it.

"Be safe," I whispered, and his chin nodded above my shoulder.

"Always."

Kyler met Cillian's hardened gaze, surprisingly keeping eye contact. It made me wonder if this particular wolf was an ex-alpha. He didn't look old enough to have already "retired," but maybe he'd had no other choice. Given his lack of fear, I might have been on to something, but I wasn't there to make new friends. It didn't seem they were, either.

Kyler spoke to Cillian directly this time, keeping his tone even. "Unless you want to go back the way you came, you're going to want to start climbing trees or braving the water. I'd recommend the trees and watch out for the snakes. They're in both places."

I swallowed thickly and thanked him for the advice once I realized Cillian was staying silent.

As soon as I was alone with my mate, I grabbed his shirt, fisting the cotton material between my fingers and pushing myself up to glare directly at him. "Quit being a dick."

"What are you talking about?" he feigned.

My mouth moved into a straight line as I waited for him to admit he'd been ruder than necessary to those guys.

In the next second, I saw the flash of fear in his eyes that had been missing since I returned from getting River.

"This is all I can be until I know you're safe." His arms wrapped around my waist, holding me against him. "You were taken from me, nearly killed, and put into harm's way more times than I can tolerate. I can't let that happen again."

He didn't say the exact words, but I'd gotten to know my mate well enough that I knew he was still blaming himself for everything that had been happening. I couldn't change his mind, but I could try to make things easier for all involved.

"Let's just try not to take any heads off until it's absolutely necessary," I said with a smile and a quick kiss.

"Should we discuss what *necessary* means to each of us?" His eyes flashed with a brief darkness.

My head shook. "You'll know. I'm sure of that."

He kissed me back, his teeth scraping over my lower lip. "I wouldn't be so sure."

Chapter Twelve

CILLIAN

There was a rage within me that I'd thought I had under control, but the moment I even thought Dawsyn was in danger...I'd been ready to kill without question. Never mind that I hadn't sensed any real threats from either of the wolf shifters. I still hadn't wanted them near my mate.

She was asking me to be kinder, but when I'd taken more time to think before, she'd been hurt. I couldn't let that happen again. I couldn't be responsible for more harm falling upon Dawsyn. I wouldn't survive that.

Protecting her, no matter who had to die in the process, was all I could offer. At least, for now.

Though, after hearing out the guards and learning that they worked under Dawsyn's family, I was attempting to find a way to understand where she was coming from.

Except having additional help didn't mean we were safe, which meant I couldn't soften the way she requested. Not until we were out of the horrid swamp and away from all the things that wanted to kill us.

Thank fuck murderous animals like the ones spoken about here didn't exist in Drago, at least in the parts nearest to town.

We began to climb trees, but we could only do that for so long or we'd never find the mushroom. I passed that thought along to Dawsyn.

"I can only focus on one thing at a time here," she said, voice confident. "Avoiding snakes and killer turtles and alligators hiding in the water holds priority until we get to another bigger patch of land."

I grinned, enjoying how unafraid she was of her weaknesses. She owned them instead of letting them own her.

"Fuck a duck!" she screeched, then slipped from the branch she was holding, but caught herself on the next one down with just one hand. "Snake. Big fucking snake."

Maybe I'd thought too soon...or she'd summoned the very thing she'd just been hoping to avoid.

"And an alligator beneath you," I growled. "Don't you fucking let go, Dawsyn."

"Wasn't planning on it, *Dear*." Her mocking tone made me think she was trying to lighten the situation, but once again, my mate was mere feet from having serious damage done to her.

I scented death before I heard the rustle of branches move. "We're not alone."

"No shi—fuck." Dawsyn must have realized I wasn't

talking about the animals, because instead of dangling herself further away from the massive python that was inching closer to her, she flung her legs up to the branch and was trying to crawl back toward me.

Only, neither of us was fast enough. I was only halfway toward her when a figure blurred into the picture, wrapped his arms around her upper half, and pulled her into the murky waters.

"No!" I roared. Any control I had over my dragon was shattered. Shifting out here wasn't ideal, but nothing was going to hurt me in my dragon form, and I needed to kill whoever thought they could touch my mate.

Though, at the last minute, I stopped the full shift, realizing if I turned into my inner beast, I would break through the branches and fall right into the water. The exact place Dawsyn had been taken into, and I couldn't risk hurting her.

I was stuck in a partial shift with my barbed wings beginning to poke out from my spine, scales covering my entire body, and my ten fingers had turned to six claws.

I leapt from the branch I was on and straight into the water. There was a glow beneath the surface, and I followed it, desperately hoping it was Dawsyn activating the powers she'd recently discovered.

Another vampire landed on my back, and his fangs tried to sink into my neck, but the scales there protected me. I was forced to stop my forward momentum to avoid bringing more of them to my mate.

My arm swung out, and I hooked the underside of

the guy's chin with my claws in my right hand. He spat and sputtered, but I wasn't going to pause.

Using the other set of claws, I raked them down his stomach, taking body parts with me as I went. I was two seconds from throwing him, but his body began to disintegrate into ash within my hold.

I dunked my hands into the water and all presence of the vampire was washed away, but there was no time for celebrating. More and more vampires were showing up, and I couldn't see Dawsyn's light in the water any longer.

Fuck. I hoped I didn't regret this.

I let the rest of my shift take over and then heard the howls. Damn it. That needed to be River and the guards coming to help and not more trouble.

Once I was fully formed into my dragon, I trudged through the water, sending streams of lightning out, not only to harm those who didn't belong, but to see where the fuck my mate was.

She was nowhere to be seen and while I couldn't afford to think she was gone...it was harder than I wanted to keep the darker thoughts at bay.

Vampire after vampire lunged at me, and it wasn't until one crawled beneath me that they finally broke skin.

The venom burned through my blood, but it didn't slow me down. Briefly, I wondered why the hell we'd hidden in another realm when the worst of these supernaturals on Earth couldn't take a single dragon down, but the potential answer wasn't something I had time for.

I rolled my body, forcing the vampire clinging to me

into the water, then slammed myself into the base of a tree until they released my scales.

Another wave of lightning left me, wrapping around the bloodsuckers, frying them to a crisp until more of them turned to ash. Just as I swung around to check for more, I heard a scream.

It sounded like it had come from Dawsyn.

My oversized body thrashed through the muddy water, uncaring what else might be in here with me, still assuming that my mate was further away based on the scream.

Branches snapped first, then trees fell over. Murky water splashed around my body, slapping against my scales, but I paid no attention to my surroundings as I destroyed everything in my path until I could finally spot my mate's glowing form.

She was back in her wolf form, chewing on the neck of one of her attackers, seeming to be in one piece.

The relief that settled deep inside me was profound. I had no idea why she'd screamed just moments before, but she appeared to be in perfect health as she ripped out the throats of her new vampire acquaintances.

Though, my reprieve was short-lived as I noticed the two guards with River gaping at my dragon just before I transformed back to two feet.

I moved out of the water and toward Dawsyn who was shifting back as well, all while keeping an eye on our two new *friends*.

Just because they worked for Dawsyn's family didn't mean we could trust them to be okay with having visual proof I was something that wasn't supposed to exist. While I didn't give a single fuck if the world knew dragons existed again thanks to me killing the vampires that wanted to harm my mate, I could go without having another situation to deal with at the moment.

River eyed both of them as I checked over Dawsyn. "Do we have a problem?"

"Not a one," Zach said first, then glanced at me. "If you ever find yourself in need of a job, I have no doubts that we will always have one for you with the protectors."

I bet they would.

If I wasn't so fucking worried about my mate's life all the damn time, it might be fun to let off some steam, occasionally hunting the idiots of this world, but I didn't see that happening anytime soon.

"So, those are the shitheads you were searching for out here," Dawsyn said.

Kyler nodded. "We get groups like that usually once a week. There isn't anything out here, so I don't know why they keep coming back."

Dawsyn looked up at me. "What if we're not the only one looking for this mushroom?"

"Then, whoever else might be is soon going to regret the choice to do so," I said, holding her tighter. "Are you sure you're okay?"

She didn't have any visible injuries, but she'd screamed, and the sound of her cry was still echoing in my mind, preventing my heart from slowing back to a normal beat.

Her head nodded against my shirt. "I pretended to be

scared to draw them in, and then my wolf ripped their heads off. It was actually kind of epic."

I glanced down at her, eyes pinched at the joy she was radiating. This woman really was unlike any I'd ever known.

"I'm glad you enjoyed yourself," I deadpanned.

She poked a finger at my chest. "You know you had fun going all dragon back there."

"When I wasn't worried about hurting you in the process, possibly a little."

"I'm fast," she reminded me with a wink that did nothing to make me think of the previous interaction as fun like she was hoping I would. "I would have gotten out of the way if your beast got too close."

"So, about the beast..." Zach said, meeting my stare head-on for the first time since I'd nearly choked him to death. "So, not a hybrid like you were trying to portray, huh?"

"No, and for the time being, it would be best if you didn't tell anyone what you saw here," I said, a deep tenor to my voice.

Kyler cleared his throat and shared a look with Zach that made me think I wasn't going to like what they had to say next.

The former pointed to the insignia on his chest. "This means something to us. I can't keep this from Maciah."

Dawsyn squeezed my hand. "I'll reach out to him and Aunt Amersyn just as soon as we're out of this swamp. They may already know, but remember what I said earlier. My family won't tell anyone unless we say it's okay, and neither will these two if they want to keep their heads."

Zach swallowed thickly, but Kyler didn't even flinch. There was a darkness about him that I didn't appreciate, but I left things alone for the moment. We had a magical mushroom to find.

"We're further into the swamp now and already covered in the rancid water," I pointed out. "Might as well take advantage and look for the plant out here."

River glanced around each of us. "We should stick together this time. Spread out a bit to cover more ground, but not out of sight from one another."

That I could agree with.

"You three fan out ahead, and we'll fill in the gaps between you all," I said, knowing that would keep me closest to Dawsyn.

Nobody disagreed and we ventured further into the swamp, out of the water and back onto the buoyant earth, liquid squishing beneath our boots with every step.

The stench around and on us was no longer insufferable, thanks to being doused in the pungent aroma, but that didn't mean I wasn't uncomfortable with my clothes sticking to me.

We'd be finding somewhere to shower and change just as soon as Ava got back to us.

Instead of staying ten-or-so feet away from me like I expected from Dawsyn, she inched back closer as we walked through the marsh. Her eyes kept glancing up at me then the ground, so I finally stopped her.

"What's wrong?" I asked.

She shrugged, avoiding my intense gaze. "Nothing."

"Don't bullshit me," I growled. "Are you hurt?"

If she'd lied to me earlier, I was going to haul her ass out of this swamp so fast that her head would spin.

"No," she answered quickly. "I was just thinking."

"About?"

She bit her lower lip. I didn't like the way my stomach churned because of that. Dawsyn was rarely nervous.

"Where we're going to live when this is all done."

That was a conversation I'd hoped to avoid for a while longer, but if the topic was causing her stress, there was no time like the present to figure things out.

Chapter Thirteen

DAWSYN

Seeing Cillian unleash his dragon abilities and realizing that the world didn't collapse the moment his energy was let free had my mind reeling with the possibilities. I hadn't forgotten that neither of us had shared what we'd want once Knox was no longer a problem.

Yet now, we were officially bonded. The thought of keeping my feelings on the matter from Cillian for too much longer wasn't sitting well with me.

"I'm intrigued by Drago," I said first.

"But?" he added with a raised brow, mouth softening.

"But my pack..."

He reached for my hand and squeezed tightly. "I know we need to be here, Dawsyn. I knew it the moment we went to Texas and I saw how affected you were by connecting to the wolves again."

I could have left things at that. He was choosing me

and my happiness and that was more than I expected, but I'd also seen him in Drago. I knew how important his home was to him. Enough that he was willing to die for it if that was the only choice.

"We can't do that," I said.

He opened his mouth with narrowed eyes, likely to disagree with me, but I continued. "Not yet, anyway."

"What do you mean?" he asked, voice laced with a bit of suspicion.

"I mean, I think once we kill Knox that our work in Drago is far from over," I said. "Your people are going to need you to rebuild, and I think they'll need me to help bridge the gap between our worlds. Things are different now. Dragons shouldn't need to stay hidden any longer."

He looked out ahead of us and I resumed scanning the ground while letting him absorb what I'd just said.

Did I think telling our supernatural communities that dragons existed would be easy? Not a chance in hell. Did I also assume they'd face some of the old problems they did before? Absolutely, but they wouldn't be alone. I'd make sure the packs stood at the dragons' side.

Plus, we had people in place like Zach and Kyler to help protect them. Not that the dragons weren't capable, but we didn't need any new wars to start, either. There could be a happy medium for everyone and death for those who couldn't follow the rules.

You're right, my wolf chimed in. *A little bloodthirsty, but right.*

Does his dragon agree? I asked.

He does, and he appreciates that you want to help their

home first, she said. *Even if the pack is where we will live out most of our years.*

I hoped it was. I'd run from my home and didn't regret that choice, because it led me to Cillian, but I no longer agreed with my reasons for taking off.

I'd always been right where I was supposed to be, and I needed to be my own person within my pack instead of trying to fit the mold of what I assumed everyone expected of me.

Sure, I'd been asked to do this or that, but most of the things I did or didn't do were because I *assumed* I had to conform or refrain as the alpha's daughter. The person I'd become, the one I'd disliked so much, was of my own making. But that didn't mean I couldn't change. I already had, and I'd show my pack the alpha wolf they'd yet to meet just as soon as the time was right.

"You're right," Cillian said another minute later. "It's time we stopped hiding. Dragons shouldn't ever feel trapped again. If I hadn't come here, we all would have died and nobody would have known until Knox showed up here to continue the destruction. What good would that have done anyone? The dangers are around us, even when we hide."

I grinned up at him, my chest filling with hope for the future that we deserved. "You'll convince the others. They'll listen to you."

"No." His eyes darkened a few shades. "They'll listen to Estelle. I might not hate her as I did just a few days ago, but this can't all be forgiven until she tells everyone the truth. She needs to share what she knows, and I'm certain she sees us on Earth."

For Cillian's sake, I hoped he could truly forgive his Nannio. The tinge of anger that still filtered through his words told me that, while their previous conversation had helped my mate out of his stupor, it hadn't healed the worst of his wounds.

Family was everything to shifters, and he'd already lost so much. Although I didn't think Estelle deserved her grandson, I'd do what I could to fix the damage done between them. For Cillian.

"So, we have a plan?" I asked. "Drago for however long we need to be there, and then to Texas when we're ready."

My father wouldn't love the first bit, but he'd get over it. Especially once I promised to come home just as soon as possible. He wasn't getting any younger, and I still had a lot to learn from him. He'd been robbed of that chance with his father, and I knew how much that still hurt his heart.

I didn't want those same pains if I could prevent them for myself.

Cillian tugged me toward him, then trailed his palms lightly over my arms. "We have a plan." He leaned forward, likely to kiss me, but I stopped him with my hand on his chest.

"If you kiss me while I reek of ass, you won't ever be able to look at me the same again," I warned him.

His chest rumbled that delicious sound I loved, and he jerked my hand out of the way. "Dawsyn."

Double fuck.

There was no stopping him this time.

His lips crashed possessively down on mine, his tongue pushing my mouth open and claiming me just like he had every right to.

He reached his fingers down until they wrapped around my thigh, pulling it up until I hooked my leg around his hips.

We were both covered in filth, more disgusting than I was pretty sure I'd ever been, but damn if I didn't want to get naked right here.

Until River shouted, "Found the mushroom!"

With a heaving chest, I broke the surprisingly intense kiss and glanced toward my best friend. He was kneeling in the marsh, face practically in the dirt. I couldn't see the bright blue color I expected from the drawing, though.

Maybe he hadn't found what he thought.

Cillian didn't let go of me, but said, "We should go see what they have."

"We should." I chuckled. "Are you going to carry me over there like this?"

His eyes sparked with desire. "I think I will."

He wrapped his arms around me, squeezing my ass with his palms. I smacked at his chest. "Put me down, you brute."

"No."

"Yes," I growled.

My mate didn't listen. Not for one second. He carried me through the swamp, groping me the ten-or-so yards it took to close the distance between us and the others.

When he stopped walking, I raised a brow. "May I get down now?"

He stayed silent for a beat, but just when I was about to dig my claws into his chest, forcing his hand, he finally released his hold. "You may."

"Overbearing beast," I muttered.

He leaned in from behind me, whispering into my ear as I started to stomp away. "You loved every second of that."

He wasn't wrong. When I reached River, I glanced at the ground and all I saw were moldy leaves from the trees above.

"What the hell have you been smoking, Riv?" I asked. "There's nothing here."

He reached for my ankle and tugged me forward. "Two small steps, then look straight down."

I did as he said, but still didn't see anything. I leaned a little further down and caught a glimmer of something glowing, but it was gone just as quickly as it appeared.

"What the fuck was that?" I asked.

"Shift forward a little, but don't step any closer," River said.

As soon as I moved my head nearer to his, the mushrooms appeared. A whole patch of the little fuckers. And they were tiny. Like only an inch tall.

"How in the world did you see those?" I asked, because if I even breathed wrong, they disappeared from my sight.

"I told you before," he said cockily. "I've spent a lot of time in the darkness, forcing my eyes to see what they shouldn't."

Cillian reached around me with the glass jar in his hand. "Your GiGi wasn't kidding about that thing being indestructible."

I hadn't even considered the jar after the fight, but there wasn't a scratch on it. Of course not.

River moved to grab it, but I stopped him. "You have to dig deep and make sure to get the roots too."

He hadn't been there when we'd received our instructions, and we couldn't afford anything else going wrong.

His eyes softened, and he held my hand gently. "I'll be careful, D. I promise."

I knew he would, but damn it. My stomach was suddenly churning. We'd already been out there too long, and I was fucking exhausted. I didn't know what I'd do if we had to keep searching, especially knowing how hard these mushrooms were to spot.

With a watchful stare, I hovered over River, making sure he sank his hands into the earth, gave a wide berth around the group of mushrooms, and moved in slowly.

"I'm going to bring as many of them up together as I can," he said quietly. "Some of them are going to break. Don't lose your shit. Most of them will be just fine."

They better fucking be.

Tension filled my shoulders, and I could hardly breathe watching River gather the precious mushrooms that I was certain laughed at me as they disappeared from my vision.

"Fuck," I hissed. "Can you even see what you're doing?" If the mushrooms disappeared at most angles, how the hell was River so sure that any of them would remain whole?

"They're not that fragile," he snarled, sliding dirt carefully into the jar. "Go punch a tree or something."

"How about your head?" I countered with a glare he didn't see as he closed the jar, holding it sideways as if it was one of those boat-in-a-bottle displays.

"We have what we need," he said, ignoring my tantrum. "Call Ava."

I grabbed my phone from my back pocket, then cursed. "It's busted." Likely from the roll in the water with the bloodsucker.

"Use mine," he said.

As I reached into his back pocket, I felt a vibration roll off Cillian from behind me. Oops. Even knowing River was like a brother to me, my mate was still more than a little possessive.

I stepped back from my best friend and pressed my back against Cillian's chest as I unlocked River's phone and found Ava's number.

My mate's fingers dug into my hips, and he breathed me in against the side of my head as I waited for Ava to pick up.

"What will you do now?" Kyler asked, he and Zach still standing close by.

"Now, we get these to Beatrix, get cleaned up, and

find the next thing the old witch needs," River replied for us just as Ava answered.

"Ready for me?" she asked instead of saying hello.

"We are," I said. "I'll send you a location pin. Be warned, we're still in the middle of the swamp, but we aren't alone. I don't want to risk trying to get these out of here and losing them."

"Fair enough. I'll be right there."

The line went dead, and I sent her the coordinates before looking at Kyler and Zach again. "Thank you for your help. I'll make sure to tell my uncle how professional you both were."

They stared at me oddly, but in their defense, I was kissing their asses a little in hopes they kept their mouths shut about my mate.

"Happy to do what we can," Zach said, then with a quick glance at Cillian and River, the protector added, "If we can do anything else, Maciah knows where to find us."

"Holy shit." Ava gagged from just a couple feet away. "You're...wretched."

A wave of magic slammed into all of us as she covered her nose and mouth. Tingles traveled over my skin and within seconds we were no longer covered in vile swamp water and smelled like literal roses.

"Hand me that," Ava demanded to River who quickly gave her the jar.

She shimmered out of appearance, but before any of us could voice an opinion about her abandoning us, she came back into view. "Beatrix has the mushrooms. She said good job. Now, you're headed to..." Her words trailed off when she noticed it wasn't just Cillian, River, and me. "Who are they?"

"Two of Maciah's men," River answered. "They helped us."

Her lips thinned. "Right. Well, we need to be going."

"Can you fix my phone first?" I asked, even though there seemed to be something up her ass tonight. I wasn't a fan of not being able to call someone if we got split up at the next location for any reason.

Reluctantly it seemed, she took the phone from my hand, placed it between her palms, muttered a few words, then tossed it back to me.

I barely had the thing back in my pocket before the witch latched onto River, then me. Thankfully, Cillian was already holding on to me because in the next second, we were gone and reappearing in a dank alley that didn't smell much better than the swamp.

"You're in New York City," Ava said. "You have an hour to get to Poppy's Pies. You need to ask specifically for Poppy. If she doesn't stab you on sight, tell her Beatrix is calling in on the favor she's owed and give her this note."

Ava shoved the paper at River but didn't let go. "Don't open that, and don't open the package she gives you. Beatrix's order."

"And we just call you when—"

She cut me off. "We're in the middle of something. Gotta go."

Mother fucking witches.

Chapter Fourteen

CILLIAN

As thankful as I was that we were out of the swamp and magically cleaned, I wasn't thrilled with being dropped off in the middle of a big city. Given I'd only been to Earth a handful of times and concentrated my destinations on supernatural ones, this was...a lot for my dragon.

It was dark—no clue what time—but it was also blindingly bright once we stepped out of the alleyway that we'd been dropped in.

Screens nearly the size of the buildings they were attached to flashed with colorful images, including nearly naked humans, food that didn't appeal to me, and random pictures and words that I assumed spilled more lies than truth.

Supernaturals weren't the only monsters that walked Earth.

The air didn't smell much better here than it had back in the swamp, but with the wind whipping around us, pushing the different scents around, it wasn't as bothersome.

"How do we find Poppy's Pies in this place?" I asked, squinting my eyes as more lights flashed around us while we stood against a store wall on the crowded sidewalk.

Dawsyn wiggled River's phone that she still had in her hand. "I'll just Goog it."

I cocked my head to the side. "You'll what?"

"Search for it on Google. You know—" She cut herself off and smiled at me sincerely. "I'm going to use the internet on my phone to find directions."

While I'd learned of the internet in my first week on Earth, I still wasn't sure everything one could find there, but I had a feeling that was better for me after the few things I did see when trying to blend in at the school.

People pushed into my back as I stood waiting for Dawsyn's direction, but I stayed my ground, becoming a wall in the sea of people.

My mate turned the phone sideways, then glanced up and down the street. "We go left."

"Is that North, East, South, or West?" River asked with a grin.

Dawsyn flipped him off and stepped forward to grab my hand. "Come on."

"Do I want to know what that was about?" I asked.

Before Dawsyn could answer, River did. "Your girl is directionally challenged."

"I am not," she snarled. "Just because when I was ten, I didn't know the meaning of those words doesn't mean I'm incapable. Asshole."

River tittered, and I held tighter to Dawsyn as we pushed through the hordes of people. My skin crawled and ears rang from all the extra noises, but I did my best to focus on my mate's touch and remember that if we didn't do this, the likelihood of my realm dying was very high.

She led the way, glancing at the illuminated screen in her hand every so often. It was only a few blocks until we came to a store with no windows and a light-pink exterior. White, wooden letters hung above the door, confirming this was indeed Poppy's Pies.

"I don't understand," River said. "This is...not GiGi's usual kind of establishment."

"No, but maybe looks are deceiving," Dawsyn said, but she didn't sound as hopeful as her words were likely meant to be. "She did mention something about pies earlier. I should have known we'd find some weird shit."

I stepped forward and opened the door first, looking inside before either of them. Everything was covered in more pink paint and white lace. It was like a young girl's bedroom, except there were glass counters filled with pastries.

A young blonde stood behind one of them. "Welcome to Poppy's Pies! We're so glad you stopped in."

Her smile stretched from ear to ear, her stance rigid yet perfect in posture, and there wasn't a wrinkle or stain to be seen on her clothes.

Dawsyn's head peeked over my shoulder. "What the fuck is this?"

I didn't know, but apparently, we were going to find out.

My mate pushed forward and went straight to the counter, not holding back any of her alpha power. "We need to see Poppy."

The robot-like...witch—I was pretty sure, but not entirely and I didn't like that—continued to smile. "Our master creator isn't available, but I'm happy to serve you. What may I have the pleasure of getting you tonight, ma'am?"

Dawsyn leaned forward and let out a vicious snarl as she slammed her fist on the counter, cracking the glass. "Not a fucking pie. Where is Poppy?"

A dark shadow fell swiftly over the blonde's blue eyes. "That was rude." Her voice was no longer saccharine, but coarse. "I said she isn't available."

"Well, make her *available*," Dawsyn practically growled, chest heaving.

I'd only seen her like this when I'd pissed her off in our early days, and while I knew I should probably intervene, I was mildly entertained. Though, it didn't seem River was.

He pushed her aside and winked at the frigid cashier. "I'm River. We came a long way, and it would be—"

He was cut off by a dark energy that caused all of our attentions to shift to the right.

A young woman with—of course—pink hair done up in pigtails and wearing a, you guessed it, pink dress stood behind Dawsyn, holding her palm within inches of my mate's face. "Who the fuck do you think you are coming into my business, making demands and damaging my property?"

She kept a smile on her face, and her voice was like the whispers of a sweet melody, but her eyes were black, and that inky darkness began traveling down her arm and toward her fingertips that were dangerously close to Dawsyn's face.

I reached for her since she hadn't moved yet, but instead, I received a laceration on my wrist. "Nope. This is my show now. Your friend here is going to pay for what she did to my counter."

The psychotic pink-haired pixie inched her fingers closer to my mate, and I lost all reasoning.

Scales burst through my skin and claws extended from my fingers. I swiped out at the young woman, but before I could make contact, she snapped her black-tipped fingers and sent me crashing into the wall behind me.

Fucking little bitch.

She pointed at me. "You're next."

"Beatrix sent us," River shouted out quickly. "Beatrix Jacobs."

Just as I was about to shift into my full dragon form and turn her precious pie shop to ash, the woman I assumed to be Poppy released whatever hold she'd had on Dawsyn and narrowly missed a punch to the face.

Poppy shook her finger in Dawsyn's face. "Quell your temper, Wolf. Why did Beatrix send you here?"

Dawsyn's lip lifted in a snarl, and she looked the young witch up and down. "*You're* Poppy?"

"*You're* the daughter of two alphas?" Poppy's tone mocked Dawsyn's. "Don't let what you see here, or anywhere for that matter, make you think you know anything, young wolf."

The pink-haired witch walked toward a set of white double doors, but I barely paid her any attention as I reached my mate, pulling her into my arms. When none of us followed, Poppy turned around. "Don't make me repeat myself more than necessary. I don't like to waste time. Come tell me why you're here."

I felt the stir of energy behind me and caught the blonde weaving her hands together, repairing the damages we'd made, a smile stitched back onto her face.

Fucking creepy.

River led the way and glanced back at us. "How about I do the talking this time?"

"What fun would that be?" Dawsyn quipped. "Dad always said you should be the strongest person in the room when arriving somewhere new. I was just showing the witch back there that she didn't scare me. It's not my fault they reacted so harshly over a stupid crack in the glass."

"Harshly?" I growled. "She was going to poison you."

She winked at me. "You're getting rather comfortable letting your dragon out here now. Don't think any of us missed that."

I wasn't under the assumption that they had, but she was right. My fucks were dwindling quickly as Dawsyn put herself in more danger.

We stepped through the double doors that Poppy had gone through, and it was as if we'd moved through a portal. In the next room, the walls were all black, and the only lights glowing were neon strings draped around us.

The thrum of heavy music moved through the air, and an invisible force pressed in around me. Breathing became difficult and the darkness inside the room took over until there was nothing left for my eyes to focus on.

I didn't panic until I no longer felt Dawsyn's hand within my grasp, but when I tried to make my dragon push to the surface, nothing happened.

"Easy there," Poppy's childlike voice sounded. "What are you?"

"None of your fucking business," I bit back.

She hummed. "Seeing as you're in my place of business, I'd say it very much is. Don't think I missed the scales on your arms just before. Are you some new hybrid shifter?"

The witch might be powerful, but she wasn't all-knowing. I was tempted to lie to her, but I was ready to be gone from this fucking city and smart enough to know we needed to comply if Beatrix was going to get what she needed to help us.

Pride be damned.

"I'm a dragon shifter," I said through gritted teeth.

"Dragons, hmmm," she cooed. "How much for your loyalty?"

"He's not for sale," Dawsyn snapped this time.

A chuckle that I assumed came from Poppy echoed around the room. "I thought I sensed a mate bond."

"We're just here to give you this letter from Beatrix," River said.

There was a beat of silence where I was still frozen in darkness, but as Poppy started to speak again, the room appeared to me once more.

She was seated in a chair, pink hair and dress standing out starkly against the black wall and throne-like chair.

"I see," she muttered, reading the letter. "You must be rather important for ol' Beatrix to use her one and only favor with me."

I wanted badly to knock this woman down a few notches but managed to keep my mouth shut as Dawsyn moved back next to me, allowing me to wrap an arm around her. I needed her touch to ground me, at least for the moment.

River stayed close as well, but just a step ahead of us. "We only need whatever she's requesting and then we'll be on our way."

Poppy's pointed brow rose, but she didn't look up from the letter. "Is that so?"

There was a soft rumble in my chest that I couldn't stop, but the witch had ceased paying attention to me. She stood once more and disappeared into the shadows further into the room.

None of us moved or spoke while she was gone, and it was several minutes before Poppy returned. She was holding a wooden box that was cracked on two sides and closed with a small, seemingly fragile latch. She handed that to River. "Tell Beatrix I'll be in touch. I rather like owing her a favor."

Just when I thought we were in the clear, the tiny witch moved quicker than I expected and grabbed my wrist, turning my arm over. "Show me again."

"No," I deadpanned.

Her grip increased and her fingertips blackened once more, but I didn't budge, which seemed to infuriate her by the pinched expression on her round face. "Yes."

"Let go of me and swear not to touch me with your magic, then I will," I said, assuming she wanted my scales just like Beatrix had before.

"Disappointing, but I guess I can just look for now," she said. "I'm happy to owe you a favor too, though."

I almost refused. Trusting her didn't seem like the best idea, but again, I wanted to get the hell out of this place and denying the witch would more than likely prevent that from happening.

My dragon energy pushed forward and the shield I'd been trying to keep up faded away with ease. The thin outline of scales appeared on my arms, and I stopped the transition, not wanting to show her too much.

Poppy's hand hovered closer. "Fascinating. Are you sure there's nothing we can trade at least?"

She was practically drooling at this point.

"I have everything I need," I said sternly, then pulled my energy back.

Her eyes snapped back up, looking at Dawsyn first then me. "I see. Now, kindly get the fuck out of my shop and don't come back, even on behalf of Beatrix, unless you're willing to trade."

That I was happy to do.

We turned around and entered back into the pink bakery. River groaned and rubbed his stomach. "I could go for some pie."

"No." Dawsyn's voice echoed in time with mine.

"Just keep that box safe until we get to the alleyway," Dawsyn added.

The blonde was back behind the register. "Thanks for visiting Poppy's Pies. Do come again."

The fuck we would.

Chapter Fifteen

Ava's glare wasn't expected when she appeared to take us back to LA. At least, not until she opened her mouth.

"You didn't even bring me a pie as a thank you for being your taxi today?" she huffed, taking the old wooden box from River. "Maybe next time think of someone other than yourself."

Her best friend, and GiGi's other right hand, Evelyn was normally the one with attitude, but it seemed as if Ava was taking on some new traits in her old age.

"Maybe next time don't send us on a treasure hunt to places that want to kill us," I retorted. "Pie was the least of our concerns."

"Says you," River muttered as Ava reached her arms out.

We held on and were gone from the disgusting streets of New York City in the next second. Only, we didn't reappear where I suspected we would.

Instead of being taken to Spell House, we were back in the coven, just beyond the tree line outside of the small community.

GiGi was already there, sitting at a small one-person table, a metal potion bottle in front of her.

"Welcome back," she said. "How was your day?"

"Rancid and unwelcome," River answered for us.

GiGi grinned. "Just as I suspected, but you were successful and you're clean now."

Ava set the box down and stepped back, folding her hands in front of us as we all watched GiGi reach for the latch.

When she twisted the small piece of rusted silver, there was a glow inside that was...pink. I shouldn't have even been surprised.

"Poppy grows very powerful flowers," GiGi explained. "She's young and obnoxious, but what she specializes in, she excels at."

My grandmother didn't give compliments lightly, but that didn't make me like the pink-haired witch after our interaction.

"This flower is the final piece we need for the syphon spell you seek," she continued. "This will solidify and strengthen everything in this bottle. Once it's opened, there is no stopping its purpose. So, don't be an idiot and use it when you're not truly ready. And if you don't *know* you're ready, then you're not."

GiGi loved calling my mate an idiot, and he took it like a champ, which I appreciated more than I'd yet to tell him. Especially since I'd threatened his Nannio behind his back. On more than one occasion.

Then again, GiGi hadn't become a traitor for "the greater good." She was just snarky.

Secretly, I was pretty sure that was everyone's favorite part about her. Though, we'd never tell her that.

She pulled the flower from the box gingerly, using both hands. Its long, thin petals were a soft pink with a neon glimmer around them, and the center was an emerald color that drew me in. Energy unlike anything I'd yet to encounter pulsed from the creation. The glow began to drip from the flower and GiGi positioned it over the potion bottle, draping the petals over the metal exterior, then pressing them down.

Underneath her hands, magic pulsed in waves and spread around us. I understood why we were out in the forest then, but not why we weren't at Spell House.

GiGi closed her eyes, her lips moving lightly as she seemed to be finalizing the spell. Seconds ticked by and once she lifted her fingers, the once-vibrant petals were shriveled and dried, as if they'd been dead for weeks.

"It's done," she said, standing from the table, legs wobbling beneath her.

Ava took a step forward at the same time I did, but GiGi snarled at both of us. "I'm fine."

Fuck. She really needed to stop being the all-powerful witch she prided herself on being. It was time for someone else to take that role on.

She handed the bottle to Cillian and held on to his hands

as he reached for it. Their stares met, and her face softened. "The whole world is counting on you, but more than that, I'm trusting you to keep my granddaughter alive. Don't make this old lady hunt you down. I will, but I'd rather not."

He nodded, moving one of his hands to her shoulder and squeezing lightly. "I would die to protect Dawsyn."

His words were earnest and pierced right through my heart before spreading through our bond.

"And that's the only reason I'm trusting you with this," she added. "Don't disappoint me. Even dead, I can make you suffer. Just remember that."

I chuckled, because I knew she was serious and it seemed that Cillian did as well.

"I won't. I promise," he said.

Once she released the metal bottle, he held it carefully between his palms, then met my gaze.

I went to his side, but I didn't stay there for long. I moved to my GiGi and hugged her tightly. "I love you and appreciate you more than I say."

She squeezed me back and didn't brush me off as I expected. "I love you, too. Now, be safe. I may not be able to help in Drago, but I did have some things left for you at the portal. I didn't figure you'd have time to get the supplies you mentioned."

After we'd gotten some sleep, I'd intended to raid the supplies in the community for things that they had plenty of, but knowing GiGi had taken care of that on my behalf made me love her even more. My heart cracked at the thought that she wouldn't always be around, but at the same time, it was so damn full of thanks for having her in my life.

"Do you want us to help you home?" I asked, knowing she needed to rest, even though she wouldn't admit it.

"No. Ava will take you back to the portal now," she said. "Call me as soon as it's done. If I don't hear from you within three days, I'll blow the whole realm to pieces."

"Thanks, GiGi." I hugged her again. "I'll talk to you soon."

River embraced her next, exchanging quiet words as I walked toward Ava with Cillian. His thumb rubbed over the back of my hand, comforting my frayed nerves, and I leaned into him.

It felt like it had been days since we'd officially bonded, yet it was only just earlier that day. I wasn't sure how that was possible, but either way, I knew I needed him now more than ever.

Not just the physical connection, but being in a place where I could take a breath and really focus on the tether between us reminded me how fucking thankful I was to have him. All of him.

"Ready?" Ava asked as soon as River joined us.

The two of us held our hands out and, in a flash, we were back at the portal. Next to the rock wall was a mountain of boxes.

The witch nodded at them. "Sorry for being short with you. Beatrix had me running boxes here and wouldn't tell me how many I had left. They just kept appearing. I think I made over a dozen trips this evening."

My grandmother was the literal best.

"Thank you, Ava," Cillian said. "I don't even need to know what's in here to know that this will make a difference to my people. Especially before we face whatever is waiting for us once we locate Knox."

That was something I hoped the others had done in our absence.

"Do you need help passing these through?" she asked, though I could hear the reluctance in her voice.

"No, you've done more than enough," I said. "Seriously, thank you."

She nodded. "I know you've said you don't need any of us to come fight, but if anything changes, we're only a call away."

The much friendlier witch disappeared before I could reply, but that didn't surprise me. GiGi's coven and community were far busier than any other in the world. I wasn't going to ask for more from them than I had to. Based on the reaction my grandmother had to the last couple spells, it might have already been too much.

"I'll step through and make sure everything is clear," Cillian said. "If it is, I'll call for Lykem and you two can pass the boxes through while he transports them."

He leaned in and kissed me before he turned to enter Drago. Just when he was going to pull away, I gripped his shirt, holding him closer a little longer and breathing him in.

Fuck. I was never going to get enough of this man.

"This will be over soon," he whispered, a promise I hoped like hell was true.

I nodded, then released him. "If you don't come back in under a minute, my wolf will tear anyone on the other side to pieces." My words were sweet, and I even winked, but I was serious.

Every time we left and came back, I became more nervous. It didn't matter that Estelle had said we had time. Shit could always change, and we'd be none the wiser. Her being a seer didn't ease my worries.

"I've already reached out to Estelle," he said. "She said something is stirring in the dark forest, but we're good to come through."

Ah, I'd forgotten about his mind link. At least he wasn't walking into a war zone. Hopefully.

My mate disappeared, and I leaned against a stack of crates, glancing at River. "How are you doing with all this?"

He moved to come stand next to me. "Not the best day I've had, but it can only get better from here, right?"

Oh, how I wished that were true, but something told me we weren't that lucky. The swamp was going to seem like heaven the moment we had to go back into the dark forest.

I took a deep inhale and then cocked my head to the side. The scent was faint, but there was something that didn't belong.

Closing my eyes, I concentrated harder.

Warlock, I thought at the same time as my wolf snarled.

The one who took River, I said to her.

We'll kill him.

That was my hope as well, but I also wanted to make sure River knew. I might have suffered in my own way, but my best friend was the one who deserved justice.

"The warlock who took you was here," I said. "He could be inside Drago right now. Shit. He might not be the only new guest."

An entire army could have crept into Drago, and I wasn't sure the dragons would be aware if there was a warlock working with them, blocking their scents.

Not unless we'd had someone stationed at the portal, but given there'd never been a reason to before, I doubted anyone had thought to do so once the restrictions were lifted.

River hadn't verbally responded, but his hardened gaze zeroed in on the portal. "I'm going to rip his body apart, limb by limb."

I looped my arm through him. "And I'll help you, but we have to be smart about this. If he's here, then that means others could be. I won't lose you to rage."

He took a shuddering breath. "No, you won't, but he's mine, Dawsyn. What he did, what you lost because of me, I need to make that right."

As much as I'd wanted to take the life of the warlock myself, I understood River. If he had the opportunity, he needed to take it.

More importantly, I'd do whatever I could to make sure he was in the perfect position to do so.

Nobody fucked with my family and got away with it.

Chapter Sixteen

CILLIAN

Once all the boxes were brought into Drago, I left them with Lykem so we could get River back to the caves. He was eyeing the dark forest with a bloodthirsty gaze that I didn't want to have to stop if he couldn't control his temper.

Dawsyn told me it was because of the warlock who had kidnapped him, and I'd also heard what she'd yet to say.

If one of them had come through, plenty of others could have as well.

I wanted to not only get River away from there, but also wanted to talk to Estelle and whoever else had been helping Lykem with the patrols.

We'd only been gone a day, but things had changed. I could feel that in the heaviness of the air around us. Even under the glow of the moon, there was a layer of something else that couldn't be seen but felt by its darkness and pressure.

"Are we good to shift?" Dawsyn asked me, also keeping a close eye on River.

I nodded. "Straight to the cave. Estelle and Mantha are waiting for us."

She paused. "Are you sure we can rely on your grandmother?"

I wasn't, but I didn't know what other choice we had. "We'll take her shared information and do what we feel is best, but we at least need to hear what they've learned today. Lykem said the groups are gathering and ready to fight, but nobody will go near the dark forest tonight. There's something out there and that probably has to do with our new guest."

Dawsyn and River both turned to look behind us, and surprisingly, it was River who shifted to his wolf form first, heading in the direction of the caves.

My mate frowned and followed her best friend's actions.

With a shuddering breath, I called my dragon forward, this time not filled with rage like the few times before. The transition was smooth and painless, the energy from my inner beast igniting me, but there was something new.

Just as I spread out my wings, my eyes zeroed in on Dawsyn.

Mate.

The word almost felt like it was said by my dragon, but it was my voice.

The bond between us had solidified back at the

coven, and as grateful as I'd been, I couldn't deny it had been a little lackluster once we'd left the confines of the cabin. There wasn't the pull or shared emotions that I expected, based on what I knew.

It was there connecting us, but also not.

Now, though...Dawsyn's wolf was like the brightest star in the sky, calling me home.

She paused just moments after I did, her wolf beginning to glow the bright silver from before. Her head turned slowly toward me and when our stares met, it was as if the world around us disappeared.

All I could sense was her love for me, the protectiveness she felt over me, River, and everyone else here even though they weren't anything to her before meeting me.

Her power radiated through me, filling my core and spreading through my body until it felt as if my dragon was growing in size.

Shit. I was pretty sure her wolf was doing the same.

What is this? I thought, not expecting an answer.

Our bond, Dawsyn's voice sounded inside my mind. *Our animals are connected. They always have been.*

You can hear me? I was already racing toward her wolf.

Hear you. Feel you. Sense every emotion. I swore her wolf smiled. *I don't think the bond was complete before as we thought, but I'd bet my life it is now.*

We met in the middle of the clearing, and I lowered my dragon to the ground. He was considerably taller than her wolf, but the need for our animals to touch was too strong to ignore, even if I wanted to have my arms around my mate and my lips on her skin.

Dawsyn's grey wolf was a bright silver by the time she got to me. Even her golden eyes glowed, and there was an intense power that radiated off her. The energy flowed from her right into me.

My wings tucked against my sides just in time for the wolf to stand next to me. With me lying down, head bowed, and her standing, our faces were almost even.

Our foreheads pressed together, and the matching rumble that came from both echoed around us, vibrating the earth beneath me. She nuzzled the side of my head, then moved to my side, curling her wolf form into my dragon.

I curled my tail around and brought my head closer to her, encasing the wolf with my body as much as I could.

I'd thought our sex had been powerful, but this was something else entirely.

It's the Luna energy in me, Dawsyn said reverently. *You're absorbing it as the power grows inside me. We're being bound together unlike anything I've ever heard of or knew could be possible.*

Out of all the surprises that had been thrown into my path since leaving Drago the first time, this was by far the most unexpected. Yet, it was also the one I was most grateful for.

We stayed there together for what felt like hours longer. No words were needed. Our emotions spoke loud enough for the two of us, and when the glow around us finally died down, I still wasn't ready to part from my mate.

Though, I quickly realized we weren't alone, and I didn't know how long that had been the case.

They wouldn't be here if they didn't have news or if there wasn't a reason to watch over us, Dawsyn said, and I regrettably agreed.

She shifted back first, and I tensed, expecting the connection between us to lessen, but the tether between us was stronger than ever before. Nothing changed, not even when I followed suit and shifted as well.

"Have a nice nap?" River asked with a wink that glinted under the moonlight. At least he wasn't bloodthirsty any longer.

"That was a bit more than a nap," Dawsyn said without an ounce of embarrassment.

"We noticed," Lykem said, standing next to River, wearing the same cocky grin.

"How long have we been out here?" I asked, entwining my fingers with Dawsyn's.

"About three hours," River answered. "When I realized you two weren't behind me any longer, I continued to the cave and helped Lykem with the crates. We came cautiously looking for you and found you two glowing together, completely unmoving. Then, your dragon appeared as if it was turning to stone. Your scales were a grey metal color for a good half hour. Creepy as fuck, by the way."

I'd never known scales to change colors like that, but

then again, being bonded to a wolf like Dawsyn wasn't something any dragon before had likely done. I thought to question the abnormality, but we'd already run out of time.

"You're welcome," Dawsyn retorted. "Well, we're done now, so let's go."

Lykem scoffed and shook his finger at my mate. "I don't think so, Wolf Girl. What the hell happened between the two of you?"

I shared a look with Dawsyn. *Should we tell them?*

Though the moment I spoke the words, I knew the mental connection we had was gone. Seemed as if that was only going to work with our animals. Unfortunate, but at least it was better than not having it at all.

She nodded at me a second later, so I assumed that even if she couldn't hear me any longer, we were both on the same page.

"Our animals completed their own bond," I said. "Dawsyn's wolf wields pure Luna energy from their Moon Goddess. It's something we saw before, but that had been diminishing as of late. With our animals bonded, that power came back in full force, and she was able to share it with me."

Lykem raised a brow. "So, you're some freaky dragon-wolf hybrid now?"

"No, but kicking your ass just became even easier."

He barked out a laugh and nudged River. "We could take them both."

"Absolutely," the wolf shifter agreed. "All day, every day."

"You two sure do know how to tell a joke." Dawsyn chuckled. "Now, tell us what's been happening?"

They shared a look I didn't like. "Estelle says their army has expanded. There is a force field that grows stronger by the hour from inside the dark forest. We don't know how many are in there or even *what* is there."

My hold on Dawsyn tightened. "I need to go see Estelle." I wasn't sure if she'd told them everything we needed to know, just like she'd failed to do before, but there was no more time for bullshit. She was going to talk to me.

Dawsyn released my hand. "Go. I'll stay with River and Lykem."

"Yeah," Lykem added with a wink. "We'll keep her safe."

Oh, that dragon would never learn.

Though, Dawsyn didn't seem to take the bait. This time.

"I'll find you as soon as I'm done." I pressed my palm to her chest. "Should be easier than before to do."

She grinned, her eyes still holding a slight glow. "No getting away from you now."

"You'd have to kill me first." I kissed her quickly, then stepped back so that I could shift. Calling my dragon forward was almost too easy. It seemed as if I went from man to beast within the blink of an eye. That had previously only happened when I was on a warpath and forcing the transition.

All eyes stayed on me as I took to the sky, knowing that I'd been right before. Time wasn't on our side.

Estelle might have thought we had three days, but I had a feeling that was no longer the case.

I flew with increased speed toward the caves, assuming that was where I'd find her, even though I hadn't arrived as quickly as I told her I would.

Much to my surprise, the first person I saw was my father. He was standing at the entrance, still appearing weak, but he was at least out of bed.

"Father," I said as soon as I shifted back and walked toward him.

"Son." He nodded curtly, his eyes still seeming too dull and skin pallor. "Did you accomplish what you needed to on Earth?"

"I did. I'm glad to see you up and getting fresh air," I replied stiffly. Fuck, this was still weird.

He coughed lightly. "It's going to be what heals me."

"Winter could also help," I pointed out. He'd thought something was going on with her, but I didn't agree. She'd done too much to help the people of Drago over the years to be a traitor of some sort.

"Yes, she could," was all he had to say.

"I need to go see Estelle," I said, not wanting the awkwardness to linger.

Yes, I was glad my father wasn't dead, but neither of us was the same person we once were. I wasn't naïve enough to think that it wouldn't be months, possibly even years, before we would have a normal relationship again.

"She's been staying in your section of the caves," he replied. "Says it's quiet there."

She wasn't wrong about that.

"Thanks, Dad."

His cheeks regained a little color. "You're welcome."

I lightly grasped his shoulder, then continued on. It was the middle of the night, but the caves were still alive with people. Though, I didn't stop to talk to anyone else. Nobody would be able to tell me what my grandmother could.

When I arrived at the back corner where I'd been sleeping, she was sitting on the ground with her head resting against her knees and her arms wrapped around her shins.

She didn't move when I stood next to her. Hell, she seemed to be barely breathing. Deciding not to disturb her in case she was seeing something helpful, I sat just a couple feet away and waited.

Her grey hair fell over her shoulders, knotted in parts, and her clothes were filthy as if she'd been on the ground ever since we'd left.

Minutes ticked by and she merely hummed and rocked back and forth every so often, but she didn't seem in pain.

When she finally looked up at me, sucking in a breath, her eyes were bright and there were tears coursing down her cheeks.

Fuck. "What's wrong?"

Her fingers swiped at her cheeks. "Nothing at all, my boy. At least, not right now."

The cracking of her voice told me whatever she'd just

seen was going to crush more than her. "Were you having a vision?"

She nodded. "The battle will happen before sunrise. Our time is up. Please tell me you have the spell."

"I do. What did you see? What have you learned?" I asked, hating the internal battle that continued to war within me.

This woman had raised me and supported me when I felt most alone. Yet, she'd put my mate in danger. I wanted to hate her. I wanted to never see her again, but the more I was around her, the more I remembered just how much she'd meant to me. Even when she was crazy.

"I'm sorry, Cillian." She reached for my hand, and I let her take it. "I'm sorry for never telling you who I really was and for not preparing you better for what was to come. You are the best thing I ever did in this life. Being your Nannio, caring for you... Don't tell your mother when you see her again one day, but you are my greatest blessing. I should have told you that more, and I'm sorry."

Emotions choked me. I didn't know what to say, but I knew right then that I could forgive her. Not only because I felt I had no choice but to accept that she'd only been doing what she thought was best, but because this was what I needed.

Absolution was what we both needed before facing Knox.

"I forgive you, Nannio," I said gruffly. "You did what you had to."

"But I could have done it differently," she said.

I quickly cut her off. "And you still can. What else have you seen? How do you know the battle is happening so soon?"

"Knox is nearly awake," she answered, still seeming more fragile than I'd ever seen her. "I didn't see them before. I didn't know they'd change everything."

"Who is they?"

Her eyes met mine, filled with grief. "The other supernaturals. There are other shifters, warlocks and witches, even vampires. They're all here, and they want to see us dead. They think they can kill Knox after helping destroy our realm. They don't understand."

No, I didn't think anyone truly did. Not even Nannio.

"We're ready." I squeezed her hand that was still gripping mine. "We'll go to them before they can come to us."

She swallowed hard. "Yes, we will. We can win this, but there will be a cost, Cillian."

"Do you see Dawsyn dying?" I asked, hoping she wasn't trying to warn me that I was about to lose what was most precious to my heart.

Her head shook, but just barely. "I can't tell you who. And I could be wrong. One decision could change everything, but we will lose even when we win. Just know that I do and always have loved you, Grandson. You're already a great man, and you're going to change not only our world, but all of them. I know this with everything I have in me."

I'd never seen her like this. Her walls were completely

down, and her crazy was nowhere to be seen. This was the woman I'd grieved when I couldn't get a hold of her. The one who had been there for me all my life, even before I lived with her.

My arms wrapped around her, and I pulled her into my side. "I love you, Nannio. Even when I was furious with you. Everything is going to be okay. I'll make sure of it."

"But if it's not okay, it's not your fault," she murmured. "Some things can't be stopped."

I didn't like what she was saying, but I knew she'd told me all that she was going to and I wasn't going to ruin the moment by forcing her hand. I didn't want that on my mind when we had a battle to prepare for.

"What do we need to do first?" I asked.

She reached behind her back and handed me a dagger in a sheath. "You need to get comfortable with this."

"I can handle a blade, but is there anything special I should know about it?" I asked, remembering she'd said before that I'd have to pierce Knox's heart with a dagger.

"It's been part of your family for several generations," she answered. "It will warm in your hand once you've done what needs doing. Other than that, nothing to concern yourself with."

Besides stabbing the man who should have been my brother in the chest.

"And we're going to need help getting to Knox," she added. "We need someone who can break the shield growing inside the dark forest. If we don't do that, we'll never get to them, and they'll pick us off one by one. Your mate needs to call on the fae. One of them will be what we need."

Possibly, but was Dawsyn going to be okay asking her family for more help than they'd already given?

Chapter Seventeen

DAWSYN

My skin itched with energy, and I badly wanted to run for miles as my wolf, but I knew that wasn't a possibility. Not until I knew what Cillian learned from Estelle.

Fuck, I hoped that conversation went well.

My mate didn't need his head filled with shit as we got ready for whatever I was sensing in the dark forest.

We're not going to have the three days we were told, my wolf said.

How do you know?

There's too much magic coming from those trees, she replied. *Something is happening soon. We need to be prepared.*

I don't think we could be more prepared even if we tried after what happened with Cillian.

Bonding with him in that new way was completely unexpected. As soon as he'd shifted, I'd known I needed him. To touch him and just be in his presence. Though, I hadn't considered that our animals would have their own unique bond.

I shouldn't have been surprised given they could speak to each other, but still.

We have full access to the Luna energy now, yes? I asked since we hadn't really discussed that yet.

We do, she replied. *I think the surge we'd had before the bonding was a glimpse of what was to come. We wouldn't have been able to handle the force of the power without Cillian. His dragon took on much of the energy for us.*

Do you have any idea what that means for him? Will his dragon be different? Will it affect his lightning abilities? I didn't want to cause more problems for my mate.

He should merely be stronger, she answered. *I've spent a lot of time since entering Drago trying to figure out why this place felt like home yet wasn't. Why Cillian had been brought to us now. I believe he needed us more than we needed him, but you would have never settled without him either. You never would have become who you were meant to be without him by your side.*

It sounded almost as if she was saying I wouldn't have been enough on my own, and as much as I cared for Cillian...that sort of pissed me the fuck off.

That's not what I'm saying at all, she explained. *He completes you and you him. You were searching for your purpose, and while we're powerful in our own right, what we are with our mate never would have come to fruition if we didn't bond with him.*

I can see that, I said, feeling a little less stabby.

Cillian was my other half. I'd yet to tell him that I loved him, but I already knew I did, and I had no doubts he knew and did as well.

My chest warmed as I focused on our bond, closing my eyes and leaning against the outside of the cave entrance. River and Lykem had gone inside to help sort through the crates. Apparently, my grandmother had provided us with medical supplies, food, clothes, and items we'd need for battle like armor and weapons for those who didn't intend to be shifted the entire time.

Though, I had a feeling the dragons were more comfortable in their animal form while fighting. I didn't blame them. Their skin was nearly impenetrable. I'd be the same way.

At least I'm fast, my wolf quipped.

The fastest, I agreed. *We make a good team in both forms.*

I truly meant that, too. I might not have always agreed with my wolf, but I knew I could trust her.

My eyes stayed closed. It was late. I didn't know what time, but it had been a long fucking day and I should have been ready for some rest. Yet, my body was still abuzz with energy from the time I'd spent with Cillian.

We rested plenty in that clearing, my wolf said.

Three hours wasn't long, but being consumed by pure Luna magic apparently made a difference.

I stayed against the wall, soaking in the heat of the rock behind me, trying to calm my mind while we waited for Cillian to return.

It wasn't long after that I sensed him getting closer and badly wished I could speak with him through my thoughts, but that didn't seem to be something that worked in our human forms.

"Dawsyn." My name rolled off his tongue with need, sending shivers down my spine that spread through the rest of my body.

There wasn't time to open my eyes before his lips were on mine and his hands moved expertly up my sides and over my shoulders, then held my face with reverence.

At least it didn't seem as if his meeting with Estelle had gone badly.

He broke the kiss but didn't pull away from me. Instead, he kept me pinned to the rocks, pressing against me as he spoke. "We're fighting tonight, and Estelle says we need a fae."

Apparently, we were getting right to the battle.

"The only fae I trust with my life just had a baby and can't help," I said. Though, that wasn't entirely true. We'd been to Fae Islands on numerous occasions growing up. Aunt Lucy had plenty of people she considered friends there; otherwise, she and Uncle Finn wouldn't have stayed.

I just didn't know any of the others there, but like the asshole I knew I could be, maybe it was better this way. If something happened to my family, I wasn't sure I could live with that. If I didn't personally know the fae...

Yeah, that was fucked up, but I owned my shitty thoughts.

"How long do we have?" I asked, already reaching for my phone.

"Nannio said we'd fight before sunrise," he answered. "So, maybe a couple hours at most. We need to break the forcefield in the forest before they're prepared to fight. Any advantage we can have we have to take."

My mate wasn't wrong about that, but as I went to reach for my phone, I remembered that my phone wouldn't work here.

"We need to go back through the portal so I can get a call out," I said.

Lykem and River strode out of the cave, not hiding the fact that they'd been listening in on our conversation. "Not necessary, Wolf Girl. Penn sorted your communication issues out. With the portal open to other supernaturals, he used some of his tech to allow calls to go through. You should have full service here."

My phone was in my grasp in the next second. Mother shit. He was right. One of the million knots in my chest loosened knowing I could speak to family anytime I needed when I was here.

"Want me to call for you?" River asked. "You know your parents love me more."

I snorted and rolled my eyes. "You only wish that were true."

Not that River didn't have the best parents. Our families were always close, even though River's lived in a different state.

My thumb pressed on my mother's name, and I brought the phone to my ear.

"Is everything okay?" She answered on the second ring.

"Hey, Mom," I replied with a smile. "Everything's fine. Mostly. I'm wondering if you're still with Aunt Lucy."

She hesitated. "I am. Why? Is the pack in trouble?"

"No, not at all," I answered. "I need a fae we can trust. Can she send someone to the portal, assuming you remember where it is?"

She'd only been there the one time that I knew of.

"Its coordinates are ingrained in my mind," she said. "I will always know where my daughter is."

I hoped not *always*, but I appreciated the sentiment.

"Don't worry Aunt Lucy too much," I said. "Give her as little detail as possible. She needs to focus on the baby. I assume they're all doing good still?"

"They are." She paused. "Why do you need a fae? That will help to know who to send."

"We need to break a forcefield within the forest here," I said. "Cillian's grandmother is a seer. We're trusting her advice that only a fae can do so."

Gods, I hoped that didn't fuck us over later, but Cillian seemed freer than I'd ever seen him. Considering we were preparing for battle...that was saying something.

"Okay, got it," Mom said. "We'll join you soon with the fae."

"No," I snapped. "We have it handled. You and Dad stay there. I'll call if things change. My phone works here now."

Her silence wasn't helping my mood.

"I mean it, Mom," I said sharply. "Do not come here."

She sighed. "I have no clue where you get your stubbornness from, but I don't like it."

I couldn't stop the laugh that escaped me. "Yeah, *no* clue. Please send the fae and text me when we should expect them."

"Of course. I love you, Dawsyn. Be careful out there."

"I love you, too. Give Dad a hug from me and everyone else."

I hung up the phone before my emotions could get the best of me.

Cillian's hand squeezed over my shoulder before sliding down my arm and tugging me toward him. He didn't say anything, but I could feel through our bond that he understood the frayed feelings within me after that phone call.

As much as I knew we needed help, I wouldn't survive the kind of guilt and grief that would follow if one or both of them were taken from us because I invited them to fight.

"Everything is taken care of inside," Lykem said. "We need to gather everyone and head toward the forest."

"Will we need to send everyone away from the cave again? People like your father can't be left defenseless," I said, glancing up at the damage from the previous fight.

Cillian shook his head. "I don't think so. Knox was getting the fire power from my father. Given we've had him this whole time, Knox shouldn't have any remnants of the stolen magic left in him to attack this far out. My father will be safe resting here while a couple of guards man each entrance to the caves."

"Not to mention you choked the life out of Knox and now he's being reborn. His energy should completely reset," Lykem added casually.

Without thought, my fist moved and connected with the snarky dragon's arm.

His hand came up, rubbing the spot as he groaned. "Rude."

"So was your comment," I clipped.

He rolled his eyes and flattened his lips. "The first bit was a joke. Cillian understands."

I glanced up at my mate, and he didn't seem entertained in the slightest.

"Right."

"So, we need to gather the dragons and head to the dark forest?" River asked, getting us back on track. "Then what?"

"Then, we hope the fae is here and we can break the shield, attacking whoever Knox has gathered before they're ready," Cillian said, his hand rubbing the back of his neck, which made me wonder if he really thought the plan Estelle had recommended would truly work.

"I'll take the wolf and gather everyone," Lykem said. "Do the two of you want to wait at the portal for the fae?"

"We can do that," I said, grabbing Cillian's hand. I wanted more time with him before the fight. It wasn't enough for me that we were bonded and had that power exchange when we'd returned from earth.

I needed my mate, and I had a feeling he needed me.

River didn't even say goodbye as he and Lykem headed around the back side of the mountain we stood before. My best friend was completely comfortable here, which made my heart happy. Selfishly.

I was already picturing him staying in Drago with me while I helped Cillian get his world back to where it was meant to be. That meant asking River to put his life on hold, and I knew in my heart I couldn't do that.

He'd been working hard to become one of the supernatural protectors. He deserved to do what made him happy and what he was clearly good at.

As Cillian and I began walking toward the portal, I expected him to want to shift since it was quicker, but he didn't seem to be in a hurry.

His hand squeezed around mine, and I took a soft inhale, briefly closing my eyes. The evening air was crisp, and the coolness of the night moved over my skin like a welcome friend. It was something I'd yet to experience in Drago.

"Are the seasons changing here?" I asked as we continued forward.

"Seasons?" Cillian's head cocked to the side.

"Like when the weather changes," I replied. "For months it might be warmer and then months it will be cooler like it is tonight."

The furrow between his brows told me we'd discovered yet another difference between our worlds.

"Drago is always like this," he said. "Well, except for when Knox was burning things to the ground it was hotter, but our evenings are always cool and days warm. Though, higher elevations do get the snow, but it melts quickly as it falls lower and runs into the river that supplies the water for everyone here."

Interesting ecosystem. His world seemed so simple when there wasn't someone trying to destroy everything within it.

We stayed quiet, walking hand in hand until he stopped us just fifty feet from the portal. Cillian's hands wrapped around my shoulders and turned me toward him.

I placed my palms over his dark-grey shirt until I could not only sense but feel the steady beat of his heart beneath my touch.

My stare found his already on my face, and our foreheads pressed together as we locked gazes, merely soaking in the presence of one another. There was a determination set in both of our faces as we stood in the open field, the dark forest waiting behind us, filled with the unknown.

"We're going to be okay," he promised. I wasn't sure if that was for my benefit or his. Maybe both.

I pressed closer to him, lightly brushing my lips over his. "We are."

His forehead stayed connected to mine, and his hand lifted until he cupped the left side of my face. "I love you, Dawsyn. With every fiber of my being. You are all I need in this world."

Without the hesitation I would have expected, I easily returned his sentiments. "I love you, too. Now and forever. No matter where we are."

We embraced tightly, a storm of emotions swirling between the two of us through the bond and filling me with a sense of determination that I didn't have before.

We had to win this fight.

A new, yet painstakingly familiar energy entered into Drago, making me stiffen in Cillian's embrace.

"No," I murmured, turning my head toward the opaque portal, hoping like hell I was wrong.

My head shook and chest expanded with frustration. This wasn't supposed to happen. Not him. Not now.

"What's wrong?" Cillian asked with a rumble in his voice and scales already appearing on his arms.

"He can't help us."

"Why?" my mate asked.

Before I could answer, Uncle Finn disappeared, then reappeared right in front of us and replied for me. "You're just as stubborn as your mother and aunt, but remember, I've lived with Lucinda for many decades now. There's nothing I can't handle."

"You just became a father," I said. "You need to go home and be with your son."

His hands cupped around my shoulders, and he leveled his blue eyes with mine. "Dawsyn, you're our niece. Did you really think that when Lucinda heard you needed help that she'd send just anyone?"

I swallowed thickly. "I'd hoped."

He gathered me into his arms. "I'm under strict

orders not to leave until you're safe. So, unless you want your aunt to show up here herself, then just accept the fact that I'm the fae you have and tell me what needs to be done."

Fuck. He wasn't wrong. I should have just been thankful that Aunt Lucy hadn't come herself. Yet, the knife I'd sworn was lodged in my chest pushed even deeper into my heart.

"If anything happens, Uncle Finn…" I trailed off, still resting my head against his shoulder.

"Do you know how many times Lucinda has tried to kill me over the years?" he asked with a light tone. "If she hasn't taken me out, then I don't think dragons will."

I wanted to point out that he'd never fought dragons, but I knew it was pointless. Instead, I steeled my emotions and pulled back from his embrace, poking a finger into his chest. "You better be okay, or I will…find you in the afterlife and make your mate seem like the nicest fae in the world."

He smirked at me. "Deal. Now, how about we head to that forest over there to break the shield you need to get through?"

I stepped to Cillian's side, and he wrapped his arm around my waist, instantly calming my tattered nerves.

"How did you know it was in the forest?" my mate asked.

Uncle Finn rubbed his palms together. "I can sense the energy. It's very dark, but I've dealt with worse before."

I'd heard the stories growing up and believed him, so I hoped Cillian did as well.

"Let's go then," he said, nudging me in that direction.

Tension filled me, weighing down on my body, slowing my heartbeat, and making every step harder than it should have been.

This was it. We either killed Knox now or... everything went to shit. No pressure.

Chapter Eighteen

CILLIAN

Our dragons were gathered, groups were put together, each one of them eager for blood. Yet, there was a chill in the air that had me on edge.

I felt confident this was where we were supposed to be and what we were supposed to be doing, but this was going to come at a cost—one I wasn't sure I was willing to pay.

With Dawsyn secured by my side, I tried to focus on the benefits of having the upper hand, but it was hard.

"Estelle is sure Knox hasn't woken up yet?" my mate asked, looking up at me briefly, then moving her stare back to her uncle as he prepared to break the shield we needed to get through.

"She said we had time," I replied, taking a deep breath.

Dawsyn said nothing in return, but I could sense her discomfort. Time didn't mean that Knox was still... coming back from the dead. We could be walking into a trap by asking Finn to break the shield, but I didn't see any other choice.

Knox had to die, and I was the only one who could do it. With the dagger Nannio had given me strapped to my hip, I gripped the hilt, eager to pierce my brother's heart with the blade.

Murder wasn't something I took lightly, especially after learning what Knox had been through growing up, but I didn't see a future in which he could change. I had to choose everyone else over the man who should have been my family.

It wasn't my, or anyone else's, fault that his father had been a psychopath.

Though, the thought that it wasn't Knox's either whispered in the back of my mind.

Every time I began to doubt what needed to be done, all I had to do was look at Dawsyn and remember what Knox had taken from us.

It didn't matter that the bond with my mate had returned. Knox had still tried to take her from me for his own gain. For that alone, he had to die. Everything else was just icing on the cake.

My chest rumbled as I pushed any sympathetic thoughts from my mind. I blamed my Nannio for them. Her openness with me had healed the hurt of her betrayal but had also made me see things differently.

That wasn't what I needed when it came to Knox.

I focused on the touch of my mate, the beat of her heart, the whisper of her breath, and the warmth she exuded as she stood next to me.

Dawsyn was my life. She always would be.

My dragon swirled within my mind, mimicking my thoughts with his own emotions.

He was stronger than ever since bonding a second time with Dawsyn's wolf. I didn't know that the animals could have their own connection, but I had no doubts within my mind that they did.

Finn's body began to glow, and Dawsyn took a step back. I angled myself in front of her. "What is he doing?"

"Showing off," she muttered with a grin.

"You only wish," her uncle replied without looking back.

"You haven't seen my wolf in action lately, Unc," Dawsyn bantered. "She may even rival my mother's."

His hands pressed together, and he closed his eyes. "You're right. The Moon Goddess has blessed you, but power isn't everything. Remember that."

Her brows pinched together at his words.

"What's wrong?" I asked quietly as Finn continued to concentrate, the pulsing of his energy growing stronger by the second.

She glanced up at me. "My wolf didn't think my new power came from the Moon Goddess. She thought it came from our bond. I know the magic we shared was Luna energy, but I guess I just assumed...I don't know."

Her eyes briefly closed, and I pulled her forward as I waited for her to elaborate. I watched her, memorizing every curve and line of my mate's face. The arch of her brows, the natural blush to her cheeks, and the plumpness of her lips. Even the angle of her jaw caught my attention, making my fingers twitch with the want of touching her smooth skin.

Her golden eyes flickered open again, and there was a peace within their depths. "It's both our bond and Moon Goddess energy that I carry. I wouldn't have had access to the power without meeting you and our bond wouldn't be what it is without the power I've inherited from my mother. The two energies seem to be working together to create something new, according to my wolf."

I brushed my fingers along her cheek, then through her brunette strands. "No matter where the power came from, you are perfect."

Through the tether connecting us, I pushed every ounce of love I had for this woman toward her, making sure there wasn't a single doubt in her mind that she was loved beyond measure and capable of anything she set her mind to.

She pushed up onto her toes and pressed her lips lightly to mine, keeping her stare locked on my eyes. "I love you, Cillian."

My forehead leaned against hers, and I gently yet firmly held her face between my palms. "I love you more than my own life."

Our shared declarations were a mere whisper in the wind, yet the emotions behind them filled me with the strength I needed to get my head right.

Knox would die. I would drive the dagger through his heart, and I would keep not only my home and people safe from his destruction, but I would make sure Dawsyn lived for many decades to come.

"Be ready," Finn shouted.

His words broke the temporary bubble around my mate and me. As Dawsyn stepped back, I noticed River and Lykem had rejoined us.

"Is everyone where they're supposed to be?" I asked.

Lykem nodded, though his eyes stayed on the fae and the forcefield around the dark forest. "Six groups of five are spread out around the shield. Everyone is shifted to their dragon forms and ready for the fight."

Dawsyn glanced up at me. "You should be in your dragon form."

I should have been, but I wanted to wait until the last minute. Being closer to her was more important to me.

"I will be," I said, then looked back at Lykem. "Thank you for getting them in place." My gaze went to River's next. "Are you sure you want to stay for this?"

He was a strong wolf, but he didn't have extra powers like Dawsyn and we had no idea what we were going to be facing once the shield came down.

His eyes narrowed, and a growl echoed from his chest. "I wouldn't be anywhere else."

I'd thought I would hate Dawsyn having a male best friend, but there wasn't a part of me that was jealous of the relationship they shared. At least not any longer.

River would die for my mate. As I wanted to find relief in that thought, I also knew she would die for him and he was, unfortunately, the weakest link here.

"Stay with Lykem," I told the wolf shifter. "I'll keep Dawsyn safe."

She scoffed. "I'll keep myself safe."

The left side of my mouth twisted upward. In that I had no doubts.

River didn't respond to my comment, and there was no time to make sure he'd heed my words.

"It's coming down," Finn called out again and I noticed the shimmering, yet nearly invisible shield was beginning to waver and crack.

The fae's forest green leather-like wings expanded from his shoulder blades and curved around him as if they were trying to press into the forcefield. As intrigued as I was about his abilities, I knew we only had seconds before I needed to shift.

I grabbed Dawsyn again and jerked her toward me more roughly than I'd initially intended. "Be fucking safe."

She kissed me with renewed vigor and smiled as if she didn't have a care in the world. "You, too. I'll shift with you."

That provided me with a minute amount of relief, knowing we'd at least be able to communicate while she was in her wolf form.

I nodded and tore myself away from her so that I could back up and transform into my dragon before it was too late.

Every foot of space created between us made my chest constrict tighter, but as I watched her swiftly shift into her wolf, the silver glow back with increasing energy, I knew everything was going to be okay.

No matter what happened during this fight, Dawsyn would be fine. She had to be. Which meant I needed to stay focused so that I could be the one standing by her side when the bloodshed ceased.

I called my dragon forward just as a wave of dark magic swept across the field we stood within. The energy felt as if hundreds of blades were slicing across my skin until my shift was complete. Even then, the heaviness in the air had my movements slower than I liked for several seconds until the pulse of the bond with Dawsyn thrummed inside me.

The power I shared with my mate grew at my core, traveling through my veins until every inch of my dragon was charged with the same energy that I'd shared with Dawsyn just hours before.

My eyes searched for her, and the soul-deep peace that pierced my heart once I found her wolf standing proud and unafraid was everything I needed to rush forward just as soon as Finn gave the all-clear.

"Go!" the fae shouted, his wings flapping and pushing himself into the sky.

My steps faltered just a few feet into the forest as I sensed something I wasn't expecting to. I didn't know how I knew, but I did without a doubt in my mind.

Knox was no longer in his regenerative state. He'd been reborn and he was ready for us.

Not only him, but dozens of dragons, witches, and warlocks awaited us as well.

We'd been lured in, but I didn't think this was a trap from my grandmother. The sincerity in her previous apology had been real. This was the best we were going to get, and we just needed to fight, not concern ourselves with how Knox had woken so early.

What was done was done, and we needed to make sure he never left this forest.

We continued to charge forward as a cohesive unit. The energy of our combined clans radiated through the air, growing with every step we took. Dawsyn's wolf ran next to my dragon, and all too soon we were faced with the opposing supernaturals.

Dragons mostly fought dragons while fending off orbs that were being thrown at us. Roars that vibrated the earth beneath us could be heard all around, fire was exchanged, and blood was shed within seconds.

It was an immediate fight to the death, and there was no turning back.

Dawsyn's wolf glowed brightly, her teeth tearing through her opponents as if their skin was nothing more than cloth. She seemed to be focused on the witches, taking as many of them down as she could so that they weren't continuing to harm the dragons.

Behind you, I shouted at her, but the attention on my mate wasn't helpful.

She was already dodging the blade of the warlock as I spoke the words, and I'd left myself vulnerable by concerning myself with her instead of those around me.

Another dragon's spiked head rammed into my side, nearly knocking me off my feet and piercing my scales.

Shit! I hissed.

Quit fucking watching me and protect yourself, Dawsyn's voice snarled inside my mind.

She was right. If I was going to keep her safe, it wasn't going to be by having my eyes on her the entire time. It would be by destroying one opposing dragon at a time.

Tapping into the new energy that flowed swiftly within my veins, I turned for the attacking dragon and unleashed my lightning power with a precision I'd yet to experience.

The rope of electricity wrapped around the pewter-colored beast, looping around his neck and tightening like a python before slithering down the rest of his body, burning through the scales.

His woeful roar echoed into the skies, but there was no one to save him. He'd chosen to give his life to Knox for whatever reason, and he would die for that choice.

I watched as the traitorous dragon burned before me, thrashing around the ground, but unable to get free from my lightning energy that continued to coil around him unlike I'd ever seen it do.

Once I was certain he wasn't getting back up, I focused my attention on searching for Knox. I could sense his presence, but I'd yet to lay eyes on him. He was hiding somewhere, watching as people died for him.

He couldn't stay hidden for long, though. I would find him, and I would end him. Soon.

Very fucking soon.

Chapter Nineteen

DAWSYN

My wolf's body was like a live wire. She was charged with energy unlike anything we'd ever experienced. Every bite, leap, and movement were enhanced as if there was nothing that could stop us.

Don't get cocky, she said. *We must stay aware and cautious.*

Oh, I was. Especially now that Cillian was no longer trying to watch my every move. He'd finally moved on and was fighting his own battles. However, through our bond, I could sense he was still distracted.

Knox had yet to make himself known, but he would soon. I had no doubts about that.

Another person I'd yet to see was Estelle.

I wanted to believe that she hadn't set us up, but considering Knox's fighters had been primed and ready the moment the shield fell, giving us the disadvantage, I was having a hard time giving the old woman any of my trust.

Are you okay over there? Cillian's voice sounded in my mind.

My wolf is ravenous and enjoying every bite, I replied, relying on dark humor as an attempt at being okay with the lives we were taking.

It was them or us. That was what I had to remember.

The tether between Cillian and me pulsed with compassion and understanding.

Though, it wasn't long before our paths took us in separate directions, and I had to put all my focus on the attackers coming for us.

My newfound abilities could only protect us from so much, and once Knox's followers seemed to realize I was more of a threat than they'd initially thought, it wasn't long before they descended on my wolf in droves.

Two warlocks and a witch came for me at once, all of them with their hands out and charcoal energy swirling from their fingertips to their elbows.

My wolf leapt for the most powerful one, a choice I agreed with, knowing that if we could lessen the threat, we stood a better chance of winning against the remaining two.

With her teeth bared and claws at the ready, she swiped at the warlock, barely grazing his black t-shirt before we were jolted with energy and pushed back.

She yelped but didn't stay down. With combined focus, we attacked again. Except, we didn't even get close enough to graze him before magic wrapped around my wolf's body, paralyzing our movements.

I slowed my breathing and kept my thoughts calm so as not to alert Cillian to my predicament .

I might not have been Luna Marked, but I still held the power of the Moon Goddess within me. These witches couldn't beat us. I wouldn't let them.

Time had been against us every step of the way, and I'd yet to truly learn what I was capable of, but trial by fire wasn't new to me.

Focus, I told my wolf.

We needed to ignore the threats around us and rely on our true source of power. I wouldn't have been given this gift if it wasn't going to save my life. That was what I was choosing to believe.

With renewed determination, my wolf relaxed, letting the dark magic around us believe it could best us. All the while, the energy at our core vibrated with a ferocity that couldn't be ignored.

Unknown to our attackers, we grew in strength as they closed in on us.

My wolf stayed prone, still enough for them to possibly even think us defeated, but that was the furthest thing from the truth.

I had a plan. In seconds, the three of them were going to be dead. That was the hope until I heard the growl of another wolf.

My wolf opened her eyes just in time for the warlock's head to be swallowed by River.

My fucking best friend.

As the body crumpled to the ground, River spit the

head out and his wolf actually freaking smiled at me as if to say, "Don't worry, D. I've got your back."

He had no idea that I'd had everything under control.

With River so close, I didn't lash out as I'd intended to, but my wolf was back on her feet in the next second and we attacked side-by-side with him.

He took on the witch next, and I was left with the remaining warlock.

While I didn't want to lash out with my full potential, I could at least protect myself better. The glow around my wolf brightened, becoming a shield of sorts. When the warlock sent a stream of dark energy at me, there was barely even a tickle against my skin.

With snapping teeth and a deep growl, we closed the distance, enjoying the way the warlock nearly tripped as he tried to back away.

Run, I dared him, even though he couldn't hear me.

He shot more magic at me, but nothing he was capable of would stop what was coming next.

Just as my wolf was prepared to go for his neck, he held his hands up, squeezing his eyes shut. "I'm sorry. I'm done. Please, don't kill me."

Mother shit.

It was one thing to take a life when that person was trying to take mine, but having someone surrender... Yet, I couldn't be too soft. The warlock had other options.

It could be a trick, my wolf said. *If he wanted to give up, he should have teleported out of here.*

I was just thinking the same thing.

The moment my wolf's eyes narrowed on the magic

user, his own gaze became nearly black and he sneered. "Burn in hell, bitch."

Our canines ripped through his neck just as he finished the insult. Blood splattered over our fur and soured in our mouth. His body fell limp, and the last thump of his heart sounded in our sensitive ears.

My wolf spit him out and stepped over the bastard without another thought. River's wolf stood nearby, frozen in place and sniffing the air.

I did the same and knew what had caught his attention.

The warlock who had kidnapped him.

He was here, just as we'd already suspected. I'd almost forgotten about River's need for vengeance, but now that it was possible, I wasn't going to rest until I made sure the fucker was dead.

I nudged River's wolf, then pointed my head to the east. I was certain that was where the warlock was.

He gave a curt nod, then led the way.

We dodged the fighting, intent on our own mission for the moment, but a dragon pushed through, separating me from my best friend. With River's mind so focused on revenge, he didn't seem to notice the distance growing between us, but that was okay.

I could handle the dragon.

Yes, we can, my wolf added as she lowered her body to the ground.

The spot where we had any real chance of hurting a dragon was their underbelly, but the risk of having them crush every bone in our body was high if the dragon decided to merely lay on us.

We not only had to be smart with our actions, but really fucking fast.

Smoke puffed out from the emerald dragon's mouth, and his clawed feet dug into the earth as he prepared to attack. His silver eyes darkened as his spiked head swiped toward me, having the advantage with his longer neck.

The sharp points barely missed skewering my wolf's side as we turned away from the beast.

She moved with effortless speed, and before I knew it, we were sliding beneath the dragon, half on our side with claws extended.

The underbelly of the dragon split apart, not enough to gush blood, but enough to piss him the fuck off.

His feet began to stomp, but my wolf had the advantage of being smaller and faster on four legs. We dodged his barbed tail and wingtips for the first few seconds, but there was nowhere to go that didn't put us in the thick of another fight.

Claws cut our back quarters before sinking into our tail. My wolf's snarl reverberated around us as she ignored the excruciating pain that traveled down our spine before spreading through too many nerves.

The dragon couldn't keep his grasp, so we escaped, barely keeping our tail mostly intact.

Fuck, that hurts, I growled, feeling her agony just as if I was in human form.

No fucking shit.

My wolf rarely cursed, so I knew she was more than

furious at having been hurt, but it didn't seem to slow her down.

We were back beneath the dragon's belly in the next second, and this time she went for blood. Lots of fucking blood.

Not only did her claws rip into his softer skin, but her teeth took their own chunk of skin out. Her head shook as she spit the bloody bits from our mouth while running out from underneath the beast.

When I tried to mentally prepare for his next move, my wolf seemed to pause in place, watching the dragon teeter.

What did you do? I asked, not understanding what was happening.

I tore his heart in two. There was no remorse in her words. No sympathy for the shifter whose eyes widened and body timbered to the ground like a large oak tree.

For a second too long, we watched to make sure he wasn't getting up again. Just when we were ready to move on—first to check on Cillian and then to catch up to River—wind whipped past us and something sharp sliced across our back.

Fuck, I hissed as my wolf's eyes turned to see who was attacking next. Only our attacker was already missing their head, courtesy of the last person I expected to save me.

Estelle turned around, dropping the witch's head to the ground. Crimson splattered across her face and hands, but what caught my attention most was the sword protruding from her chest.

"You couldn't die," she murmured, her body swaying forward.

I shifted back to human form within a second and caught her body with both hands before she could fall. "Estelle, don't you fucking die."

"Had to save you." Her words were garbled, and blood trickled from the corner of her mouth.

Mother fucking shit.

My hands moved over her chest, ripping her shirt away to inspect the wound. If I could find Winter, Estelle could be healed. She couldn't be worse off than Lykem had been before. Not from one stab wound.

That's not just a stab wound, Dawsyn, my wolf said solemnly.

I knew she was right, but I was trying to believe that the blade had missed Estelle's heart and this wasn't as bad as it looked.

"Take care of my grandson," she said in a strangled whisper. "Tell him I'm sorry."

"Tell him yourself," I demanded, holding her tighter, but it didn't matter how much I didn't want her to die for me.

Her chest stuttered, and then she was limp in my hold, eyes partially open, but unseeing.

My knees grew weak, and I lowered us to the ground. *Damn it! I can't just leave her here.*

We need to keep fighting, my wolf replied, her sympathy oozing into me.

I need to find Cillian, I said. *He can't find her body like this.*

Let's go then.

Though, I couldn't head back in the other direction until I had eyes on River. Two quick scans of the bloodied battlefield and I found his wolf. His auburn fur was covered in gore and within his jowls was the head of a warlock that deserved so much worse than what I assumed was a quick death.

Good fucking riddance, I thought as my best friend spit the head to the ground and continued on without even a limp to his steps.

He was okay, and now I needed to make sure my mate was as well.

We couldn't lose anyone else.

Chapter Twenty

CILLIAN

I'd stayed close to Dawsyn as long as I could, but when the scent of Knox grew too strong to ignore, I found myself heading deeper into the forest, shifting back to my human form for stealth.

Just like before, something twisted in my chest. We'd already walked right into one trap when the shield fell, and it was likely Knox was more prepared for me than I was for him, but I couldn't let him get away.

Nannio had made it clear that this was our one shot. I had to end Knox during this fight. The consequences of not doing so were too great to even consider another option.

So, trap or not, I continued to follow the scent of the dragon that should have been my brother and best friend, keeping my fingers wrapped lightly around the hilt of the dagger that would officially end his life.

My dragon stirred inside me, staying close to the surface and ready to burst free at a moment's notice. I'd have stayed shifted if I thought my dragon capable of stabbing Knox in the heart, but I knew this was a task I had to do myself.

I had to look him in the eyes and take his life.

Without question, I knew I could and would do it, but that didn't mean it was easy.

I also had the syphon spell in my pocket, but Beatrix made it clear that I wasn't to use it until I was absolutely certain it was time.

"Hello, Brother," Knox's voice echoed around me, making it difficult to know what direction the sound originated from.

"Funny that you call me 'Brother' so easily, yet you've done nothing to treat me as family," I replied, focusing my senses and searching for his heartbeat.

"Thanks to your traitorous grandmother, I'm sure you've learned by now that my views on family are vastly different from yours."

I hoped he wasn't trying to garner sympathy from me. Was there a part of me that felt sorry for him for all he'd gone through? Of course. I wasn't a monster, but that changed nothing.

Knox would die by my hand.

A branch snapped to my left, then another on the right, but those weren't the sounds I was focused on. It was the soft, slow beat of Knox's heart that I'd finally picked up on that led me forward.

He appeared from behind a tree, hiding in the shadows, but I had no problems seeing his face and dark eyes.

Very little of his appearance reminded me of myself or even my mother. His cheeks were sharper, and there was a coldness about him that I'd never be able to replicate, even on my worst day.

"Do you intend to kill me, Brother?" he taunted, leaning against the bark of the tree, seemingly without a care in the world.

"There's a lot I intend to do." Drawing this out and prolonging the inevitable wasn't one of those things, though.

My fist shot out with more power and speed behind the punch than ever before. Even still, Knox's skin seemed to harden under the impact, and he barely budged when I connected with his chin.

His taunting laugh echoed around us. "You've changed since I last saw you. Maybe I should have kept your mate a little closer while I had the chance."

My teeth ground together, but I wasn't going to let him push me into doing something before I was ready. I knew I couldn't just take Knox's life. Not like before.

He'd changed as well, and I wouldn't rush into anything, getting myself killed in the process.

A glow began to illuminate from behind him, growing around his back before spreading around his entire body.

"Our mother was a whore who deserved to die," he snarled.

"Your father was a psychopath who should have died long before he did and you know it," I returned. There was no scenario in which Knox didn't understand his dad was a monster.

He stepped closer, fiery red scales appearing on his arm, nothing like the charcoal and emerald I'd seen on him before. "At least he never left me for dead."

"And neither did my mother," I said, mimicking Knox's footsteps. "Your *father* tricked her. She didn't know you were an Ember dragon when he killed you in front of her." I wasn't sure what he planned next, but I was going to be ready.

There was a flash of doubt within his dark eyes, but he blinked the weaker emotion away. "Lies!" His shout was followed by the ricochet of lightning energy reaching out from his scales, wrapping around the trees and then heading right for me.

Assuming his abilities were still similar to mine, I dropped to the ground, rolling several feet back before looking back up.

The tendrils of burning energy collided, sparking and flaming for a couple of seconds before turning to smoke.

I leapt to my feet and charged for Knox. My dragon pushed forward, and I channeled the half-shift that I'd done when we were in the swamp.

My body grew taller, and my skin was protected by scales. My chest heaved as I charged forward, drawing out my own lightning energy and lashing out at him.

The white strands of power wrapped around his still-glowing body but fizzled out just as quickly as they'd appeared.

"You can't beat me, dear brother," he called out,

brushing the back of his hands over his shoulder as if he was flicking away dust. "I am the future. This world is the past, and I will be the ember that burns this wretched place to the ground and scorches the Earth until only those loyal to me are left."

He was capable of those things. In that, I had no doubt, but it wasn't going to fucking happen.

"If only all that power could make you see the truth." I charged forward once again, claws out and ready to strike. His face was exposed, the only part of him not covered in scales and the reddish glow.

With speed unlike I'd ever had, I swiped, cutting his ear clear off and through his left cheek before backing up.

One hit at a time to weaken him before I opened the syphon spell. Beatrix's magic could take away his shield, and then I would pierce his heart with the dagger.

I just had to keep fighting.

His responding roar shook the earth beneath my feet. "You'll fucking pay for that."

Just as I anticipated, Knox unleashed more lightning, but this time, with it came dark energy unlike anything I'd ever felt before.

While I was capable of dodging the initial blasts, the darker shadows that followed weren't as easy to evade.

A black cloud enveloped me, stealing the breath from my lungs and burning my insides as it pushed itself through my body.

I tried to cough and expunge the darkness, but that only put me on my knees.

Knox's fiery glow appeared in front of me and

kneeled just enough to wrap his hand around my throat and lift me back up.

His other hand pointed to his head, where his ear was already regrowing. "You can hurt me, but you can't beat me. What will it take for you to understand that?"

The darkness around me—seeming to resemble smoke, based on the lack of air I was able to breathe—only grew heavier. I didn't have long before my bodily functions would slow too much for me to do what needed to be done.

I'd thought I needed to weaken Knox, but that wasn't going to happen. Not any longer.

With forced and shaky movement, I reached my fingers toward my pocket. Except my actions didn't go unnoticed.

Knox released my neck and kicked me in the ribs on my way to the ground. I gasped, losing more air I didn't have to give and landed on my side.

"You can't beat me!" he shouted, but it seemed as if he was trying to convince himself more than he was me.

I couldn't deny that I truly did feel sorry for him, but again, that changed nothing.

His boot landed several more hits to my stomach, and while the impact hurt, my scales absorbed the worst of the pain.

I closed my eyes, trying to appear defeated as I lay on my side. My hand reached into my pocket once more, this time taking hold of the syphon spell.

Just as I was about to flick the lid open and hope that would be good enough, the bond with Dawsyn darkened. She was hurting, which had my entire body frozen in fear.

I'd left her and she was hurt. Again.

My dragon rumbled inside me, and I heeded his warning, focusing closer on the bond.

My mate wasn't wounded. She was grieving.

Fuck. If something happened to River…

I couldn't think about that now. All I had to focus on was making sure she didn't have to lose anyone else today.

Knox kicked me again, this time the momentum pushing me onto my back. I wanted to say something to distract him, but no words would leave my mouth as breathing became impossible for me.

He kneeled over me, pressing his hands over my neck. "Fitting I should take your life just like you did mine, don't you think?"

That wasn't going to fucking happen.

With my hand still shoved in my pocket, my fingers twisted the lid to the potion bottle, and I hoped like hell I wasn't fucking up by opening it while it was still in my pants.

A blackness flickered at the edges of my vision, threatening to take over completely, but I fought against the darkness that would take all the pain away. I had to keep fighting.

For my mate. For my home. For myself.

Seconds ticked by. Knox pressed harder against my neck, his nails breaking through my skin and so close to tearing my throat out.

Was the syphon spell not going to work? Was I too late?

My eyes fluttered closed against my will, and Knox's laugh of victory was like throwing gasoline on an already blazing inferno.

"Give up, Brother," he whispered. "You…"

His sentence trailed off just as my body went slack, losing all fight. A quiet calmness entered my mind, and I breathed a sigh of relief.

Wait…

That had been a literal sigh. Like I could fucking breathe again.

My arms were slow to move, and the weight of Knox was still over me, but the acid in my lungs was fading.

Even the thrum of my bond to Dawsyn was pounding inside me with renewed vigor, growing brighter by the second and filling me with a strength I knew could only come from my mate.

I opened my eyes to find Knox frozen in place over me. His scales were fading, and the red glow that had been protecting him was nowhere to be seen.

My fists pushed him off me, and he tumbled to the ground. I reached for the dagger still strapped to my side and ripped it from the sheath.

The silver blade glinted under the moonlight directly above, and I positioned myself, ready to strike.

Yet, I paused.

What the fuck was wrong with me? He had to die. Right the hell now.

But the thought that he was still my brother filtered through my mind.

I shook my head.

No.

He was nothing to me. Not family or even friend.

He was the bastard who stole my mate. Killed my uncles. Burned my town.

He had to fucking die.

Still, as I watched him lay there defenseless, I couldn't force my arms to drop down and pierce his heart.

"I'm fucking crazy."

"No, you just have a better heart," my mate's soft voice whispered from right behind me.

She wrapped her arms around me, placing her hands over mine. "It's him or us, and we can't kill him any other way. I knew the moment Estelle said you had to be the one to stab him that this would be hard. Not because you're weak, but because of the incredible man you are."

As she spoke into my ear, her arms pushed further down, guiding the dagger over Knox's heart.

Dawsyn was right, and I hated that it still didn't change anything for me.

Though, maybe it did, because I didn't fight against her. I let her help me in this moment, to be there for me.

As the tip of the dagger rested just over his chest, she lifted her hands. "You have to do this, Cillian. Before the syphon spell runs out."

My eyes briefly closed, and when I reopened them, I could see Knox's skin start to take on an orange hue. If I didn't act, there was a chance I'd never finish this.

With my mate behind me, hand pressed between my shoulder blades and her warmth soaking into me, I knew I couldn't let anything live that threatened her and the future we deserved.

Knox, brother or not...fucked up situation or not... had to cease existing.

I focused my eyes on his slack face and cloudy stare. "I wish you peace, Brother."

The blade pierced his skin with resistance, but I didn't let up. I pushed harder on the hilt, driving the dagger through Knox's heart and watching his face the entire time. He had been raised by a shitty fucking father and had done unforgiveable deeds, but he would not die alone.

I stayed with him as the orange faded and he began to gasp for breath, no longer under the hold of the syphon spell.

His head turned toward me, and our stares locked on one another. For the first time, his eyes softened toward me. No words were spoken as the time ticked by.

Knox closed his eyes, and the last thump of his heart sounded like a siren in my mind.

He was gone.

The nightmare was over. Yet, it didn't feel as if anyone had won.

Chapter Twenty-One

DAWSYN

The moment I'd heard the deep roar come from further within the forest, I'd known my mate was in trouble. When our bond began to flicker, I swore my heart had stopped, and when I finally found them with Knox choking the life out of my mate...

I'd been two seconds from losing my shit until my wolf stopped me. My emotions had been so frayed that I hadn't noticed the fading of the black smoke around Cillian and the way Knox's shoulders began to stiffen.

It's the syphon spell, she'd told me.

I couldn't see it right away, but as Cillian's chest began to rise and fall normally and the tether between us regained its strength, I found the will to let him do what needed to be done on his own.

This was Cillian's task. Estelle had given him the dagger, and I wasn't going to get in the way, even though taking Knox's life after what he'd done to me sounded like a dream.

As I watched Cillian hesitate and felt his sorrow through our bond, I knew then that my mate was too good for this world.

He was strong and could be ruthless when needed, but he cared with every fiber of his being.

Learning who Knox truly was, how he'd grown up, and what had been done to him had changed something for Cillian.

I hadn't wanted to see it then, but it was clear as day as I watched from the shadows of the trees.

When I knew my mate was struggling, I didn't hesitate in joining him, wrapping my arms around his and reminding him of the stakes.

"It's him or us and we can't kill him any other way. I knew the moment Estelle said you had to be the one to stab him that this would be hard. Not because you're weak, but because of the incredible man you are."

My hands pushed his further down as I spoke, until the dagger was grazing Knox's chest and it was time for me to pull back. "You have to do this, Cillian. Before the syphon spell runs out."

I could already see Knox fighting against GiGi's spell. He was just as strong as Estelle had warned us he would be. Cillian had to do this now.

With bated breath, I waited several more seconds for the dagger to pierce Knox's heart once and for all.

After the task was complete, Cillian leaned back against me and I anchored myself to the ground, keeping us both upright.

"It's okay," I whispered against his neck. "He's free from the pain now."

There was no doubt in my mind that Knox had become the person he was because of the trauma he'd experienced. Regardless of his father telling him that he could rule the world, it was the abuse Knox had been subjected to that turned his soul black.

Though he'd had a choice to be better, he chose not to be, which was why there was no ache in my heart at seeing his lifeless body on the ground before us.

The only ache I still held was for Cillian's grandmother. I didn't want to tell him she was gone, but he gave me little choice in the matter.

"What happened out there?" he asked gruffly. "Is River or Lykem..."

I shook my head against his shirt. "Not them."

"Dawsyn, your uncle. Fuck, I'm so sorry."

As far as I was aware, Uncle Finn was perfectly fine. Though, the mention of those I cared about made me want to run back toward the fight I hoped was now over.

"It's not my family, Cillian." I held him tighter, wishing my strength could take away the sorrow I knew he was about to be consumed with.

"Nannio," he murmured, shaking within my hold.

"I'm sorry," I said softly. "She saved me. Took a sword that was about to be driven through my back."

"She was better than we gave her credit for," he replied, voice cracking, but in the next second, he was pulling away from me and standing. He reached a hand to me. "We need to go and finish this. Nobody else can die. I won't let her sacrifices be for nothing."

He was right. There would be time to grieve later.

I let him pull me against his chest, and when I expected him to start running back toward the fight, his face came closer to mine and he kissed me until my toes curled and I was gripping tightly to his shirt.

His tongue swept across my mouth, and I opened for him easily, tasting him and grounding myself with our bond.

Only seconds later, he was pulling away, but I didn't complain. He was right. We had to check on the others.

Together, we ran back toward the fight. To my disappointment, it was still going, but the battles were fewer and farther between, and there wasn't a single warlock or witch to be seen.

Hopefully the fuckers had all had their heads ripped from their shoulders.

I turned to tell Cillian where his grandmother was, but he grabbed my arm, shoved me to the ground hard, and roared so loudly my ears rang.

"What the fu—" I stopped mid-sentence when I turned over to find Cillian's fist inside the chest of a warlock.

Apparently, they weren't all dead. Until now. Hopefully.

My mate yanked his hand back, bloodied and holding what I could only assume was the man's heart before he shoved the warlock to the ground and tossed the organ on top of his dead body.

Cillian's chest was heaving. The grief he'd been feeling just moments before had turned to full-on rage. Thanks to our bond, his ire was so strong that I was beginning to feel the drive to stab someone.

"Dawsyn!" The familiar voice made my heart sink.

I turned slowly to find my mother covered in blood and limping.

My body swayed, and I blinked slowly. How bad was she hurt? Where was my father? How many of them had come?

I couldn't move. Not until my wolf spoke.

She's okay. Look to her left.

I did and found my father's wolf running to catch up with my mother.

Thank fuck.

My hand gripped my chest as I tried to ease the momentary anxiety, then I ran to close the distance between my mother and me.

"You're not supposed to be here," I hissed when I got my arms around her.

"When Finn didn't return quickly, there was no way we were staying behind," she replied gruffly. "Lucinda brought us."

"She didn't leave—"

Mom shook her head. "She didn't even cross through the portal."

I pulled back in time to see my father shift, then I fell into his arms. "Dad."

He hugged me so tightly that breathing was

nonexistent for several seconds. "The thought of losing you was..."

"I'm okay," I promised, pulling back and checking on the other fights.

Cillian's dragon was out in full force, his lightning energy lashing out at those who refused to stand down and ending the last of the battles with little effort.

"You have one hell of a mate," Mom said with a slight grin.

My heart filled with pride. "That I do."

Next, I caught Uncle Finn helping River walk toward us. It seemed as if my best friend was about to lose a damned arm. "Winter!" I screamed probably much louder than was necessary.

A faint, "Be right there" sounded from behind us as I ran toward them.

River grinned. "You should see the other guy."

"A dragon nearly took your arm off, River," I chastised.

He winced as Uncle Finn settled him onto a patch of earth that wasn't covered in blood. "It'll heal."

I wasn't so sure about that, especially when Winter looked him over with wide eyes and shaking hands. "This is going to be...painful. Bite me, and I'll make sure the scar will scare women away from you for years to come."

As Winter began to work her healing magic on my best friend, Uncle Finn inched closer to her. "You're...fae."

"What?" Cillian demanded, seemingly appearing out of nowhere.

"She's half-fae," Finn said. "Her energy is much like my sister's. Though they do different things, I know what I'm sensing."

"That shouldn't be possible," my mate muttered.

Winter stayed quiet, and I wondered if she'd already known, but now wasn't the time to interrogate her. At least Cillian's dad wasn't crazy in saying there was something off about her. He'd sensed what none of us had.

I reached for Cillian, thankful his emotions were calmer and he seemed to be more in control. "Where is Lykem?" Not that I didn't care for the lives of the other dragons. I just didn't want my mate to hurt worse than he already was.

"He's helping secure those who surrendered," Cillian answered, then nodded at my father. "Lykem said you saved his life when you showed up. Thank you."

"You can count on the wolves to help whenever you need it," my father replied. "Even if you have stolen my daughter from me."

Mom elbowed him in the ribs. "Enough."

Dad winked at me, then wrapped an arm around his mate and said, "Yes, Dear."

I shook my head at their antics, then glanced at Cillian. "The fight is over?"

He nodded and pulled me into his arms. "Fucking finally."

My heart warred with relief and sorrow. So many lives were lost, but we had somehow survived. And like my father had shared with me many times growing up, even when battles were won, there were never any winners.

I'd thought I understood his words before, but it wasn't until right then that I truly felt them, deep in my soul.

Epilogue

DAWSYN

One Year Later

My wolf raced through the forest, breathing hard and running faster than I was certain we'd yet to go. The further we went, the higher the elevation became and the harder it was to breathe, but still. Every time we were out in trees and mountains, we pushed and pushed until we couldn't go any further.

Even then, we gave just a little more effort.

I'm not sure why you consider this fun, Cillian's voice sounded in my mind.

Because one day it will save my life, I replied. *Plus, we need to remain the fastest wolf in all the realms. I have a reputation to maintain.*

My mate wasn't pleased I had a "reputation" at all,

but it wasn't long after the battle that word had spread about our fight and the realm we'd saved.

All with Cillian's permission, of course.

His dragon flew over us, landing just fifty feet ahead.

My wolf skidded to a stop, and before either of us could shift back, our two animals pressed their heads together, seeming to enjoy their silent communication.

In all the months, she'd never shared with me what she and the dragon spoke about, but her love for him only grew with each passing day. Just as mine did for Cillian.

Finally, I was back on two feet, and within seconds, my mate was scooping me up into his arms. His head buried into my neck. "You smell different."

I grinned even though he couldn't see my face. "I'll be in heat soon."

That had him freezing within my hold. "A heat, you say…"

I'd been through one other since knowing Cillian and hadn't been ready before, but I'd known what was coming for the last week and had already decided it was time for us to start trying for a family.

After all he'd lost and with all I hoped for in the future, there was no time like the present.

Cillian pushed me back until he could see my face. "Do you want to have a baby?"

With everything we'd had to do in the last year to make the transition of dragons being accepted on Earth again, there hadn't been time before. We hadn't been ready, but considering Drago had been rebuilt twice as quickly as any of us had expected, thanks to the help of the fae and witches, I couldn't find a reason to wait.

I nodded and grinned even bigger. "I've been thinking about it."

"Fuck, Dawsyn," he murmured my name deeply. "It's all I can think about."

Even though I'd had a feeling he'd be on the same page as me, as we so often were, a tsunami of relief still rushed through me at his confirmation.

There was only one caveat that I wasn't sure he'd be okay with.

"But I'd like to raise our child with the wolves," I said. "Not that I haven't enjoyed our time here and getting to know your world. It's just not the same as having a pack."

Cillian had lost all of his blood family aside from his father, who was finally back to full health and running Drago as if he'd never been gone.

There were still clans, but they didn't come together like the packs did. Knowing our child would be a hybrid created from two powerful shifters...I needed him or her to have all the protection possible. At least until they could protect themself.

Cillian stroked my face with the back of his fingers and smiled gingerly at me. "Oh, Mate. You have no idea what I've been up to, do you?"

I cocked my head to the side. "What do you mean?"

"Those trips I've made back to Earth by myself to play liaison for the dragons with the other supernaturals," he said. "Those weren't all business."

"I'm sorry, what?" My words were laced with a growl that wasn't because I was angry with my mate, but because I'd somehow missed him doing something that sounded rather important.

"I've been to your pack a dozen times in the last couple months," Cillian explained. "With everyone back in their own homes and my father in full health, I knew it was only a matter of time before we left. Roman has been helping me get a place ready for us. Everything is already set up. We can leave whenever you want."

I threw my arms around his neck and squeezed tightly. "And here I thought I couldn't love you more." My lips pressed against his neck, then moved back to his face until I could see his eyes again. "But this is our home, too. We can spend time here as often as you need."

His hands slid gently over my back, holding me flush against him. "Home for me is wherever you are, Dawsyn. I need for nothing else besides you to be at my side, happy and healthy."

Fuck. My heart was going to stop working if he continued to say shit like that to me.

"You better get me indoors before I get naked," I returned and was in his arms before I could take my next breath.

"Your wish is my command." The smirk on his face said he was getting exactly what he'd hoped for, but so was I, so I didn't give a single damn.

Not as long as I had my mate.

Three Years Later

"I swear to the Moon Goddess, if I step on another toy, I'm going to burn them all," I snarled as I rubbed the arch of my foot.

"Sorry, Momma," Ethan muttered, toddling over to me. "Want a kiss?"

Damn it. He was his mother's son, and I couldn't stay irritated for long.

My hand mussed his short brunet hair. "No, Son. Just try to help Momma keep the living room clean."

"O-tay." He began picking up after himself, and I leaned further into the cushions.

Have kids, I'd said. Get the mothering out of the way before it was time for me to be alpha.

What the fuck had I been thinking? I thought as I glanced down at my protruding stomach, knowing that my out-of-control hormones were the only reason I was so pissy about the fucking toys.

I hadn't even been hurt.

Thankfully, our son was just as much of a saint as his father was and never held my mood swings against me.

My hand moved over my belly, feeling our little girl move. "Hopefully, you'll be the same."

Then I snorted, because according to my mother, I was doomed to produce another stubborn alpha female.

The thought made my smile grow. I was ready for her. We all were.

"Where's my favorite nephew?" River's voice carried through the house as I heard the door slam closed.

"Here! Here!" Ethan shouted, already running toward his uncle.

I stayed put on the couch. Eight months pregnant with our second pup. It would take a lot more than my best friend to get my ass up.

River entered the living room, carrying my son and laughing. "I hear there will be a toy sacrifice soon."

"Quite possibly," I replied casually. "What are you doing here?"

He put a wiggling Ethan back on the ground, then grasped at his chest dramatically. "Can't a guy just want to see his best friend? Man, maybe I should come back later."

I ignored his pouting as he sat next to me on the couch, throwing an arm around my shoulders and reaching for my stomach. "How's my favorite niece today?"

"You know when you say 'favorite' that it holds no meaning given they're your only nephew and niece?"

River glared at me. "They don't understand that. Let me have my glory."

I could maybe do that.

"She's ready to come out," I said, finally answering his question. "And I'm ready for that as well. I'm not sure what I was thinking having two kids so close together. I'm never going to sleep again."

"As your best friend, it's my duty to remind you of your previous words when several of us told you not to rush kids." He paused, then straightened, flicking invisible hair around his shoulders and adding an unnecessarily high pitch to his voice. "I'm the alpha heir, and I want to be a mother before I have to choose between my family and my pack. Leave me the fuck alone."

My sneer was deep, and the corresponding growl even deeper. "First, I don't sound like that. Secondly, I still believe that. I'm just..."

"Tired, growing a pup, hungry, twice your normal size," he started to tick off all very valid reasons for my crankiness, but I dug my nails into his thigh at the 'twice your normal size' comment. Even if it was the truth.

"Shut the fuck up, River."

Ethan gasped. "Momma has a poopy mouth."

My best friend at least had the decency to cover his laugh with his hand.

"Sorry, Son," I muttered, pushing myself up from the couch. "Momma needs food."

River followed me to the kitchen. "Let me make you something while I tell you why I'm here."

I pointed at him with a glare. "I knew you were here for more than a visit."

He'd been working out of town a lot as a protector even though he'd already proven himself time and time again. He was supposed to have a permanent spot here in Texas, working alongside Lykem who was still training to be a protector but staying within the pack. Unfortunately, not everyone was accepting dragons as easily as we'd hoped.

River shrugged, getting out all the makings of a sandwich. "I'm here for a visit as well."

Sure, he was.

As he prepared the sandwiches in silence, I stared him down until he finally cracked. "Justine needs me."

I raised a brow. "The vampire you swear you don't have a thing for?"

Over the years, I'd teased River relentlessly that he should just cave and hook up with our mutual friend, but he'd refused.

Not that he'd been celibate, but he was convinced he'd find his mate soon enough and never allowed himself to get too close to another woman besides me.

Well, and Justine. She'd remained one of our closest friends, and I didn't like hearing she needed help.

"Isn't she back in New York with her nest?" I asked when Riv didn't take my bait.

He nodded, sliding me a turkey sandwich, then taking his and sitting next to me at the table. "She is, and wants to leave for good this time, but it seems as if her nest leader isn't keen on letting her go easily."

That sounded messy.

"Have you talked to Maciah and Amersyn?" They were his bosses and our family and also vampires. I knew they'd help if they could.

"I did, but they're stretched thin with dragon integrations."

Of course they were, because people were still shitty and every dragon that wanted to move to Earth had to have a personal guard with them that reported any threats for the first six-to-twelve months they were here.

I wasn't surprised by it, but that didn't mean I wasn't annoyed as fuck.

"What can I do?" I asked, no longer interested in my food.

"You can make sure my niece is brought into this world with ease and let me know when it's time for me to cut the cord. Cillian can't have all the fun."

"The hell he can't," my mate yelled from the backside of the house.

River frowned. "I swore he wasn't here."

"*He* is always here," Cillian said as he entered the kitchen, kissing me first, then pointing at River. "You're not getting anywhere near my mate while she delivers. Not after last time."

I grinned, remembering the entertaining day. My water had broken, GiGi was nowhere to be found, and my three favorite men were losing their shit.

Between my dad yelling at everyone within a ten-foot radius, Cillian looking like he was going to pass out, and River crying *then* passing out, I hadn't even cared about the contractions.

Cillian took a bite out of my sandwich, then began rubbing my shoulders and neck. "I can help with Justine if you need it."

"Let me see what's going on for myself and I'll let you know," River said, somehow already finishing his lunch and pushing away from the table. "I need to go. Thanks for the food. And I mean it, don't have my niece without me."

River blew me a kiss and said goodbye to Ethan before he was on his way.

While I'd done a lot of complaining about being pregnant again and was disappointed that I couldn't help our friend, I knew River could handle whatever was happening.

Deep down, I knew I was exactly where I was supposed to be.

In my pack, with my family, and creating the home I'd never thought I could have here.

"Not that I don't enjoy when you're happy, but care to fill me in on what's causing the elation I'm sensing from you, Mate?" Cillian asked, his lips so close to my ear that his teeth scraped against the sensitive skin of my lobe.

My hand raised, reaching for him as I turned around. "You, our home, our babies, the pack, everything we've worked and sacrificed for. All of it makes me the happiest alpha in all the realms."

He lifted me into his arms, cradling my body against his. "All those things make me happy, too. Except maybe the babies. They've cut into my mate time."

The grin on his face told me he was joking, but he wasn't wrong. I'd missed my mate on numerous days, even when we slept in the same bed.

"Maybe we need to call his grandparents and tell them they're overdue for a sleepover with their grandson," I said, running my hand over his chest, then up his neck.

"That just might be the best idea you've ever had," he

said, then called for Ethan. "Pack a bag, Son. You're sleeping at the pack house tonight."

A jubilant "yay" echoed from the living room, and my heart expanded to the point of being the best kind of painful thanks to all the love and want I could feel from Cillian through our bond.

Things might not have been perfect in every sense, but they were perfect for us.

No matter what the future held or what problems we faced, I knew true happiness. That was more than I could have ever hoped for.

Thank you for reading the final The Hidden Realm book! If you haven't read the other series in this world featuring some of your favorite characters, flip the page for more info!
In the meantime, join me in my reader group Heather Renee's Book Warriors to stay updated on all the things!

Mystics and Mayhem

If this is your first trip into the Mystics and Mayhem, welcome! Hello again, if not :) For our first timers, the series you're reading—The Hidden Realm—is technically the start of the second phase within Mystics and Mayhem and the fifth series within this world!

Check out the list of all the Paranormal Romance stories included in this world below. Ones where you'll always find fierce, yet relatable leading ladies and strong alpha males who sweep them off their feet, along with humor and intrigue that will keep you turning the pages.

While you don't have to read the series in any particular order as there are no spoilers between each trilogy, this is the recommended reading order:

Broken Court (Lucinda and Finn)
Dark Fae Cursed — Dark Fae Freed — Dark Fae
Unrivaled

Boxed Set with Bonus Content
Luna Marked (Cait and Roman—Dawsyn's Parents)
Wolf Kissed — Wolf Taken — Wolf Mated
Boxed Set with Bonus Content
Scorned by Blood (Amersyn and Maciah)
Vampire Heir — Vampire Ash — Vampire Vow
Boxed Set with Bonus Content
Fated to the Wolf (Andie and Foster)
Shifted Magic — Altered Magic — Forged Magic
Boxed Set with Bonus Content
The Hidden Realm (Dawsyn and Cillian)
A Dragon's Wolf — A Dragon's Curse — A Dragon's Fate

Now I know I mentioned about that this series was the start of the second phase and while I have several more stories ideas to draw from... I need the readers to tell me that want me to continue with Mystics and Mayhem.

Let me know with your reviews, posts, by sharing with friends, or any other way, including shouting it from the rooftops ;) If I don't believe enough readers want more, I'll move on to a new world, which I have no doubt will be just as epic as this one.

Though, I'm also content to stay right here.

In the meantime, if you want to stay up to date on all the bookish things, or have any questions, join my reader group Heather Renee's Book Warriors on Facebook or send me an email anytime at HeatherReneeAuthor@ yahoo.com.

I hope you enjoy this world as much as I have!

Find Heather on Facebook:
Reader Group
Want to talk all things books and get updates before anyone else? Come hang with me in my reader group:
Heather Renee's Book Warriors

Author Page
Teaser and big updates are also posted here:
Heather Renee Author

Newsletter:
I send this out sporadically, so don't worry. You won't ever be spammed by me and you get a couple goodies when you sign up!
http://smarturl.it/HeatherReneeNL

MYSTICS AND MAYHEM SERIES

Broken Court

A complete New Adult Urban Fantasy series featuring an unconventional and anti-heroine leading lady, a broody love interest, and a fae kingdom with a vile king.

Luna Marked

A complete New Adult wolf shifter series (dual POV) featuring a strong-willed leading lady and a patient, yet fierce alpha male.

Scorned by Blood

A complete New Adult Vampire series featuring a supernatural hunter and the sexy vampire bound to protect her no matter the cost.

Fated to the Wolf

A complete New Adult Witch and Wolf series (dual POV) featuring an abandoned witch, a rogue wolf, and their broken bond.

The Hidden Realm

A Complete New Adult Wolf and Dragon series (dual POV) featuring an alpha female intent to set her path in life and the dragon shifter who isn't going to let her get away without a fight.

Raven Point Pack Series

A complete Upper Young Adult Paranormal Romance series featuring wolves, witches, vengeance, and fated mates.

Shadow Veil Academy

A complete Upper Young Adult Urban Fantasy Academy series featuring shifters, elves, witches, and more.

Elite Supernatural Trackers

A complete New Adult Urban Fantasy series featuring witches, demons, a smart-mouthed female lead, alpha males, and a snarky fairy sidekick.

Royal Fae Guardians

A complete Young Adult Urban Fantasy series featuring fae, magic users, a sweet romance, along with snark and humor.

Blood of the Sea Series

A complete Young Adult Paranormal Romance series featuring vampires, open seas adventures, and the occasional pirate.

STANDALONE BOOKS

Ignite Me - A spicy wolf shifter story featuring a lost heir, the mate who doesn't want her, and the enemies who wish them dead.

Marked Paradox - A Young Adult fae story about a realm divided and one fae to bring them back together.

About the Author

Heather Renee is a USA Today Bestselling author who lives in Oregon. She writes Paranormal Romance and Urban Fantasy novels with a mixture of romance, humor, and sass. Her love of reading eventually led to her passion of writing and giving the gift of escapism.

When Heather's not writing, she's spending time with her loving husband and beautiful daughter, going on their own adventures. She loves to hear from her fans, so visit her website: www.HeatherReneeAuthor.com and check out the Contact Me page for ways to connect.

www.ingramcontent.com/pod-product-compliance
Lightning Source LLC
Chambersburg PA
CBHW061544210726
48287CB00006B/2074